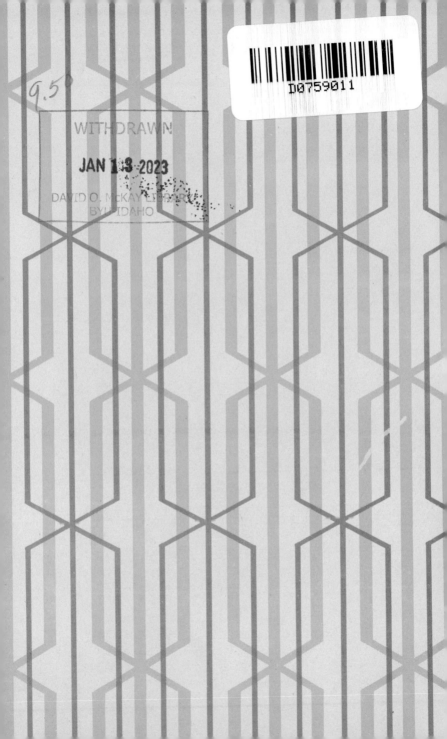

The Lady of the Barge

HE DENIED IT AGAIN, HOTLY.

THE LADY
OF THE BARGE

By
WILLIAM WYMARK JACOBS

I L L U S T R A T E D

Short Story Index Reprint Series

 BOOKS FOR LIBRARIES PRESS
FREEPORT, NEW YORK

First Published 1902
Reprinted 1969

STANDARD BOOK NUMBER:
8369-3203-X

LIBRARY OF CONGRESS CATALOG CARD NUMBER:
75-101815

MANUFACTURED
BY
HALLMARK LITHOGRAPHERS, INC.
IN THE U.S.A.

CONTENTS

LIST OF ILLUSTRATIONS

The Lady of the Barge

THE LADY OF THE BARGE

THE master of the barge *Arabella* sat in the stern of his craft with his right arm leaning on the tiller. A desultory conversation with the mate of a schooner, who was hanging over the side of his craft a few yards off, had come to a conclusion owing to a difference of opinion on the subject of religion. The skipper had argued so warmly that he almost fancied he must have inherited the tenets of the Seventh-day Baptists from his mother while the mate had surprised himself by the warmth of his advocacy of a form of Wesleyanism which would have made the members of that sect open their eyes with horror. He had, moreover, confirmed the skipper in the error of his ways by calling him a bargee, the ranks of the Baptists receiving a defender if not a recruit from that hour.

With the influence of the religious argument still upon him, the skipper, as the long summer's day gave place to night, fell to wondering where his own mate, who was also his brother-in-law, had got to. Lights which had been struggling with the twilight now burnt bright and strong, and the skipper, moving from the shadow to where a band of light fell across the deck, took out a worn silver watch and saw that it was ten o'clock.

Almost at the same moment a dark figure appeared on the jetty above and began to descend the ladder, and a strongly built young man of twenty-two sprang nimbly to the deck.

"Ten o'clock, Ted," said the skipper, slowly.

"It 'll be eleven in an hour's time," said the mate, calmly.

"That 'll do," said the skipper, in a somewhat loud voice, as he noticed that his late adversary still occupied his favourite strained position, and a fortuitous expression of his mother's occurred to him: "Don't talk to me; I've been arguing with a son of Belial for the last half-hour."

"Bargee," said the son of Belial, in a dispassionate voice.

"Don't take no notice of him, Ted," said the skipper, pityingly.

"He wasn't talking to me," said Ted. "But never mind about him; I want to speak to you in private."

"Fire away, my lad," said the other, in a patronizing voice.

"Speak up," said the voice from the schooner, encouragingly. "I'm listening."

There was no reply from the bargee. The master led the way to the cabin, and lighting a lamp, which appealed to more senses than one, took a seat on a locker, and again requested the other to fire away.

"Well, you see, it's this way," began the mate, with a preliminary wriggle: "there's a certain young woman——"

"A certain young what?" shouted the master of the *Arabella*.

"Woman," repeated the mate, snappishly; "you've heard of a woman afore, haven't you? Well, there's a certain young woman I'm walking out with I——"

"Walking out?" gasped the skipper. "Why, I never 'eard o' such a thing."

"You would ha' done if you'd been better looking, p'raps," retorted the other. "Well, I've offered this young woman to come for a trip with us."

"Oh, you have, 'ave you!" said the skipper, sharply. "And what do you think Louisa will say to it?"

"That's your look out," said Louisa's brother, cheerfully. "I'll make her up a bed for'ard, and we'll all be as happy as you please."

He started suddenly. The mate of the schooner was indulging in a series of whistles of the most amatory description.

"There she is," he said. "I told her to wait outside."

He ran upon deck, and his perturbed brother-in-law, following at his leisure, was just in time to see him descending the ladder with a young woman and a small handbag.

"This is my brother-in-law, Cap'n Gibbs," said Ted, introducing the new arrival; "smartest man at a barge on the river."

The girl extended a neatly gloved hand,

shook the skipper's affably, and looked wonderingly about her.

"It's very close to the water, Ted," she said, dubiously.

The skipper coughed. "We don't take passengers as a rule," he said, awkwardly; "we 'ain't got much convenience for them."

"Never mind," said the girl, kindly; "I sha'nt expect too much."

She turned away, and following the mate down to the cabin, went into ecstasies over the space-saving contrivances she found there. The drawers fitted in the skipper's bunk were a source of particular interest, and the owner watched with strong disapprobation through the skylight her efforts to make him an apple-pie bed with the limited means at her disposal. He went down below at once as a wet blanket.

"I was just shaking your bed up a bit," said Miss Harris, reddening.

"I see you was," said the skipper, briefly.

He tried to pluck up courage to tell her that he couldn't take her, but only succeeded in giving vent to an inhospitable cough.

"I'll get the supper," said the mate, suddenly; "you sit down, old man, and talk to Lucy."

In honour of the visitor he spread a small cloth, and then proceeded to produce cold beef, pickles, and accessories in a manner which reminded Miss Harris of white rabbits from a conjurer's hat. Captain Gibbs, accepting the inevitable, ate his supper in silence and left them to their glances.

"We must make you up a bed, for'ard, Lucy," said the mate, when they had finished.

Miss Harris started. "Where's that?" she inquired.

"Other end o' the boat," replied the mate, gathering up some bedding under his arm. "You might bring a lantern, John."

The skipper, who was feeling more sociable after a couple of glasses of beer, complied, and accompanied the couple to the tiny forecastle. A smell compounded of bilge, tar, paint, and other healthy disinfectants emerged as the scuttle was pushed back. The skipper dangled the lantern down and almost smiled.

"I can't sleep there," said the girl, with decision. "I shall die o' fright."

"You'll get used to it," said Ted, encouragingly, as he helped her down; "it's quite dry and comfortable."

He put his arm round her waist and squeezed her hand, and aided by this moral support, Miss Harris not only consented to remain, but found various advantages in the forecastle over the cabin, which had escaped the notice of previous voyagers.

"I'll leave you the lantern," said the mate, making it fast, "and we shall be on deck most o' the night.   We get under way at two."

He quitted the forecastle, followed by the skipper, after a polite but futile attempt to give him precedence, and made his way to the cabin for two or three hours' sleep.

"There'll be a row at the other end, Ted," said the skipper, nervously, as he got into his bunk. "Louisa's sure to blame me for letting you keep company with a gal like this. We was talking about you only the other day, and she said if you was married five years from now, it 'ud be quite soon enough."

"Let Loo mind her own business," said the

mate, sharply; "she's not going to nag me. She's not *my* wife, thank goodness!"

He turned over and fell fast asleep, waking up fresh and bright three hours later, to commence what he fondly thought would be the pleasantest voyage of his life.

The *Arabella* dropped slowly down with the tide, the wind being so light that she was becalmed by every tall warehouse on the way. Off Greenwich, however, the breeze freshened somewhat, and a little later Miss Harris, looking somewhat pale as to complexion and untidy as to hair, came slowly on deck.

"Where's the looking-glass?" she asked, as Ted hastened to greet her. "How does my hair look?"

"All wavy," said the infatuated young man; "all little curls and squiggles. Come down in the cabin; there's a glass there."

Miss Harris, with a light nod to the skipper as he sat at the tiller, followed the mate below, and giving vent to a little cry of indignation as she saw herself in the glass, waved the amorous Ted on deck, and started work on her disarranged hair.

At breakfast-time a little friction was caused by what the mate bitterly termed the narrow-minded, old-fashioned ways of the skipper. He had arranged that the skipper should steer while he and Miss Harris breakfasted, but the coffee was no sooner on the table than the skipper called him, and relinquishing the helm in his favour, went below to do the honours. The mate protested.

"It's not proper," said the skipper. "Me and 'er will 'ave our meals together, and then you must have yours. She's under my care."

Miss Harris assented blithely, and talk and laughter greeted the ears of the indignant mate as he steered. He went down at last to cold coffee and lukewarm herrings, returning to the deck after a hurried meal to find the skipper narrating some of his choicest experiences to an audience which hung on his lightest word.

The disregard they showed for his feelings was maddening, and for the first time in his life he became a prey to jealousy in its worst form. It was quite clear to him that the girl had become desperately enamoured of the skipper, and he racked his brain in a wild effort to discover the reason.

With an idea of reminding his brother-in-law of his position, he alluded two or three times in a casual fashion to his wife. The skipper hardly listened to him, and patting Miss Harris's cheek in a fatherly manner, regaled her with an anecdote of the mate's boyhood which the latter had spent a goodly portion of his life in denying. He denied it again, hotly, and Miss Harris, conquering for a time her laughter, reprimanded him severely for contradicting.

By the time dinner was ready he was in a state of sullen apathy, and when the meal was over and the couple came on deck again, so far forgot himself as to compliment Miss Harris upon her appetite.

"I'm ashamed of you, Ted," said the skipper, with severity.

"I'm glad you know what shame is," retorted the mate.

"If you can't be'ave yourself, you'd better keep a bit for'ard till you get in a better temper," continued the skipper.

"I'll be pleased to," said the smarting mate. "I wish the barge was longer."

"It couldn't be too long for me," said Miss Harris, tossing her head.

"Be'aving like a schoolboy," murmured the skipper.

"I know how to behave *my*-self," said the mate, as he disappeared below. His head suddenly appeared again over the companion. "If some people don't," he added, and disappeared again.

He was pleased to notice as he ate his dinner that the giddy prattle above had ceased, and with his back turned toward the couple when he appeared on deck again, he lounged slowly forward until the skipper called him back again.

"Wot was them words you said just now, Ted?" he inquired.

The mate repeated them with gusto.

"Very good," said the skipper, sharply; "very good."

"Don't you ever speak to me again," said Miss Harris, with a stately air, "because I won't answer you if you do."

The mate displayed more of his schoolboy nature. "Wait till you're spoken to," he said, rudely. "This is your gratefulness, I suppose?"

"Gratefulness?" said Miss Harris, with her chin in the air. "What for?"

"For bringing you for a trip," replied the mate, sternly.

"*You* bringing me for a trip!" said Miss Harris, scornfully. "Captain Gibbs is the master here, I suppose. He is giving me the trip. You're only the mate."

"Just so," said the mate, with a grin at his brother-in-law, which made that worthy shift uneasily. "I wonder what Loo will say when she sees you with a lady aboard?"

"She came to please you," said Captain Gibbs, with haste.

"Ho! she did, did she?" jeered the mate. "Prove it; only don't look to me to back you, that's all."

The other eyed him in consternation, and his manner changed.

"Don't play the fool, Ted," he said, not unkindly; "you know what Loo is."

"Well, I'm reckoning on that," said the mate, deliberately.   "I'm going for'ard; don't let me interrupt you two.   So long."

He went slowly forward, and lighting his pipe, sprawled carelessly on the deck, and renounced the entire sex forthwith.   At teatime the skipper attempted to reverse the procedure at the other meals; but as Miss Harris steadfastly declined to sit at the same table as the mate, his good intentions came to naught.

He made an appeal to what he termed the mate's better nature, after Miss Harris had retired to the seclusion of her bed-chamber, but in vain.

"She's nothing to do with me," declared the mate, majestically.   "I wash my hands of her. She's a flirt.   I'm like Louisa, I can't bear flirts."

The skipper said no more, but his face was so worn that Miss Harris, when she came on deck in the early morning and found the barge gliding gently between the grassy banks of a river, attributed it to the difficulty of navigating so large a craft on so small and winding a stream.

"We shall be alongside in 'arf an hour," said the skipper, eyeing her.

Miss Harris expressed her gratification.

"P'raps you wouldn't mind going down the fo'c'sle and staying there till we've made fast," said the other. "I'd take it as a favour. My owners don't like me to carry passengers."

Miss Harris, who understood perfectly, said, "Certainly," and with a cold stare at the mate, who was at no pains to conceal his amusement, went below at once, thoughtfully closing the scuttle after her.

"There's no call to make mischief, Ted," said the skipper, somewhat anxiously, as they swept round the last bend and came into view of Coalsham.

The mate said nothing, but stood by to take in sail as they ran swiftly toward the little quay. The pace slackened, and the *Arabella,* as though conscious of the contraband in her forecastle, crept slowly to where a stout, middle-aged woman, who bore a strong likeness to the mate, stood upon the quay.

"There's poor Loo," said the mate, with a sigh.

The skipper made no reply to this infernal insinuation. The barge ran alongside the quay and made fast.

"I thought you'd be up," said Mrs. Gibbs to her husband. "Now come along to breakfast; Ted 'll follow on."

Captain Gibbs dived down below for his coat, and slipping ashore, thankfully prepared to move off with his wife.

"Come on as soon as you can, Ted," said the latter. "Why, what on earth is he making that face for?"

She turned in amazement as her brother, making a pretence of catching her husband's eye, screwed his face up into a note of interrogation and gave a slight jerk with his thumb.

"Come along," said Captain Gibbs, taking her arm with much affection.

"But what's Ted looking like that for?" demanded his wife, as she easily intercepted another choice facial expression of the mate's.

"Oh, it's his fun," replied her husband, walking on.

"*Fun?*" repeated Mrs. Gibbs, sharply. "What's the matter, Ted."

"Nothing," replied the mate.

"Touch o' toothache," said the skipper. "Come along, Loo; I can just do with one o' your breakfasts."

Mrs. Gibbs suffered herself to be led on, and had got at least five yards on the way home, when she turned and looked back. The mate had still got the toothache, and was at that moment in all the agonies of a phenomenal twinge.

"There's something wrong here," said Mrs. Gibbs as she retraced her steps. "Ted, what are you making that face for?"

"It's my own face," said the mate, evasively.

Mrs. Gibbs conceded the point, and added bitterly that it couldn't be helped. All the same she wanted to know what he meant by it.

"Ask John," said the vindictive mate.

Mrs. Gibbs asked. Her husband said he didn't know, and added that Ted had been like it before, but he had not told her for fear of frightening her. Then he tried to induce her to go with him to the chemist's to get something for it.

Mrs. Gibbs shook her head firmly, and boarding the barge, took a seat on the hatch

"YOU VILLAIN!" SHE SAID, IN A CHOKING VOICE.

and proceeded to catechise her brother as to his symptoms.   He denied that there was anything the matter with him, while his eyes openly sought those of Captain Gibbs as though asking for instruction.

"You come home, Ted," she said at length.

"I can't," said the mate.   "I can't leave the ship."

"Why not?" demanded his sister.

"Ask John," said the mate again.

At this Mrs. Gibbs's temper, which had been rising, gave way altogether, and she stamped fiercely upon the deck.   A stamp of the foot has been for all time a rough-and-ready means of signalling; the fore-scuttle was drawn back, and the face of a young and pretty girl appeared framed in the opening.   The mate raised his eyebrows with a helpless gesture, and as for the unfortunate skipper, any jury would have found him guilty without leaving the box. The wife of his bosom, with a flaming visage, turned and regarded him.

"You villain!" she said, in a choking voice.

Captain Gibbs caught his breath and looked appealingly at the mate.

"It's a little surprise for you, my dear," he faltered, "it's Ted's young lady."

"Nothing of the kind," said the mate, sharply.

"It's not? How dare you say such a thing?" demanded Miss Harris, stepping on to the deck.

"Well, you brought her aboard, Ted, you know you did," pleaded the unhappy skipper.

The mate did not deny it, but his face was so full of grief and surprise that the other's heart sank within him.

"All right," said the mate at last; "have it your own way."

"Hold your tongue, Ted," shouted Mrs. Gibbs; "you're trying to shield him."

"I tell you Ted brought her aboard, and they had a lover's quarrel," said her unhappy spouse. "It's nothing to do with me at all."

"And that's why you told me Ted had got the toothache, and tried to get me off to the chemist's, I s'pose," retorted his wife, with virulence. "Do you think I'm a fool? How dare you ask a young woman on this barge? How dare you?"

"I didn't ask her," said her husband.

"I s'pose she came without being asked," sneered his wife, turning her regards to the passenger; "she looks the sort that might. You brazen-faced girl!"

"Here, go easy, Loo," interrupted the mate, flushing as he saw the girl's pale face.

"Mind your own business," said his sister, violently.

"It is my business," said the repentant mate. "I brought her aboard, and then we quarrelled."

"I've no doubt," said his sister, bitterly; "it's very pretty, but it won't do."

"I swear it's the truth," said the mate.

"Why did John keep it so quiet and hide her for, then?" demanded his sister.

"I came down for the trip," said Miss Harris; "that is all about it. There is nothing to make a fuss about. How much is it, Captain Gibbs?"

She produced a little purse from her pocket, but before the embarrassed skipper could reply, his infuriated wife struck it out of her hand. The mate sprang instinctively forward, but too late, and the purse fell with a splash into the water. The girl gave a faint cry and clasped her hands.

"How am I to get back?" she gasped.

"I'll see to that, Lucy," said the mate. "I'm very sorry—I've been a brute."

"*You?*" said the indignant girl. "I would sooner drown myself than be beholden to you."

"I'm very sorry," repeated the mate, humbly.

"There's enough of this play-acting," interposed Mrs. Gibbs. "Get off this barge."

"You stay where you are," said the mate, authoritatively.

"Send that girl off this barge," screamed Mrs. Gibbs to her husband.

Captain Gibbs smiled in a silly fashion and scratched his head. "Where is she to go?" he asked feebly.

"What does it matter to you where she goes?" cried his wife, fiercely. "Send her off."

The girl eyed her haughtily, and repulsing the mate as he strove to detain her, stepped to the side. Then she paused as he suddenly threw off his coat, and sitting down on the hatch, hastily removed his boots. The skipper, divining his intentions, seized him by the arm.

"Don't be a fool, Ted," he gasped; "you'll get under the barge."

The mate shook him off, and went in with a splash which half drowned his adviser. Miss Harris, clasping her hands, ran to the side and gazed fearfully at the spot where he had disappeared, while his sister in a terrible voice seized the opportunity to point out to her husband the probably fatal results of his ill-doing. There was an anxious interval, and then the mate's head appeared above the water, and after a breathing-space disappeared again. The skipper, watching uneasily, stood by with a life-belt.

"Come out, Ted," screamed his sister as he came up for breath again.

The mate disappeared once more, but coming up for the third time, hung on to the side of the barge to recover a bit. A clothed man in the water savours of disaster and looks alarming. Miss Harris began to cry.

"You'll be drowned," she whimpered.

"Come out," said Mrs. Gibbs, in a raspy

voice. She knelt on the deck and twined her fingers in his hair. The mate addressed her in terms rendered brotherly by pain.

"Never mind about the purse," sobbed Miss Harris; "it doesn't matter."

"Will you make it up if I come out, then," demanded the diver.

"No; I'll never speak to you again as long as I live," said the girl, passionately.

The mate disappeared again. This time he was out of sight longer than usual, and when he came up merely tossed his arms weakly and went down again. There was a scream from the women, and a mighty splash as the skipper went overboard with a life-belt. The mate's head, black and shining, showed for a moment; the skipper grabbed him by the hair and towed him to the barge's side, and in the midst of a considerable hubbub both men were drawn from the water.

The skipper shook himself like a dog, but the mate lay on the deck inert in a puddle of water. Mrs. Gibbs frantically slapped his hands; and Miss Harris, bending over him, rendered first aid by kissing him wildly.

Captain Gibbs pushed her away. "He won't come round while you're a-kissing of him," he cried, roughly.

To his indignant surprise the drowned man opened one eye and winked acquiescence. The skipper dropped his arms by his side and stared at him stupidly.

"I saw his eyelid twitch," cried Mrs. Gibbs, joyfully.

"He's all right," said her indignant husband; "'e ain't born to be drowned, 'e ain't. I've spoilt a good suit of clothes for nothing."

To his wife's amazement, he actually walked away from the insensible man, and with a boat-hook reached for his hat, which was floating by. Mrs. Gibbs, still gazing in blank astonishment, caught a seraphic smile on the face of her brother as Miss Harris continued her ministrations, and in a pardonable fit of temper the overwrought woman gave him a box on the ear, which brought him round at once.

"Where am I?" he inquired, artlessly.

Mrs. Gibbs told him. She also told him her opinion of him, and without plagiarizing her husband's words, came to the same conclusion as to his ultimate fate.

"You come along home with me," she said, turning in a friendly fashion to the bewildered girl. "They deserve what they've got—both of 'em. I only hope that they'll both get such awful colds that they won't find their voices for a twelvemonth."

She took the girl by the arm and helped her ashore. They turned their heads once in the direction of the barge, and saw the justly incensed skipper keeping the mate's explanations and apologies at bay with a boat-hook. Then they went in to breakfast.

The Monkey's Paw

THE MONKEY'S PAW

I.

WITHOUT, the night was cold and wet, but in the small parlour of Laburnam Villa the blinds were drawn and the fire burned brightly. Father and son were at chess, the former, who possessed ideas about the game involving radical changes, putting his king into such sharp and unnecessary perils that it even provoked comment from the white-haired old lady knitting placidly by the fire.

"Hark at the wind," said Mr. White, who, having seen a fatal mistake after it was too late, was amiably desirous of preventing his son from seeing it.

"I'm listening," said the latter, grimly surveying the board as he stretched out his hand. "Check."

"I should hardly think that he'd come to-night," said his father, with his hand poised over the board.

"Mate," replied the son.

"That's the worst of living so far out," bawled Mr. White, with sudden and unlooked-for violence; "of all the beastly, slushy, out-of-the-way places to live in, this is the worst. Pathway's a bog, and the road's a torrent. I don't know what people are thinking about. I suppose because only two houses in the road are let, they think it doesn't matter."

"Never mind, dear," said his wife, soothingly; "perhaps you'll win the next one."

Mr. White looked up sharply, just in time to intercept a knowing glance between mother and son. The words died away on his lips, and he hid a guilty grin in his thin grey beard.

"There he is," said Herbert White, as the gate banged to loudly and heavy footsteps came toward the door.

The old man rose with hospitable haste, and opening the door, was heard condoling with the new arrival. The new arrival also condoled with himself, so that Mrs. White said, "Tut, tut!" and coughed gently as her husband entered the room, followed by a tall, burly man, beady of eye and rubicund of visage.

"Sergeant-Major Morris," he said, introducing him.

The sergeant-major shook hands, and taking the proffered seat by the fire, watched contentedly while his host got out whiskey and tumblers and stood a small copper kettle on the fire.

At the third glass his eyes got brighter, and he began to talk, the little family circle regarding with eager interest this visitor from distant parts, as he squared his broad shoulders in the chair and spoke of wild scenes and doughty deeds; of wars and plagues and strange peoples.

"Twenty-one years of it," said Mr. White, nodding at his wife and son. "When he went away he was a slip of a youth in the warehouse. Now look at him."

"He don't look to have taken much harm," said Mrs. White, politely.

"I'd like to go to India myself," said the old man, "just to look round a bit, you know."

"Better where you are," said the sergeant-major, shaking his head. He put down the empty glass, and sighing softly, shook it again.

"I should like to see those old temples and fakirs and jugglers," said the old man. "What was that you started telling me the other day about a monkey's paw or something, Morris?"

"Nothing," said the soldier, hastily. "Leastways nothing worth hearing."

"Monkey's paw?" said Mrs. White, curiously.

"Well, it's just a bit of what you might call magic, perhaps," said the sergeant-major, off-handedly.

His three listeners leaned forward eagerly. The visitor absent-mindedly put his empty glass to his lips and then set it down again. His host filled it for him.

"To look at," said the sergeant-major, fumbling in his pocket, "it's just an ordinary little paw, dried to a mummy."

He took something out of his pocket and proffered it. Mrs. White drew back with a grimace, but her son, taking it, examined it curiously.

"And what is there special about it?" inquired Mr. White as he took it from his son, and having examined it, placed it upon the table.

"It had a spell put on it by an old fakir," said the sergeant-major, "a very holy man. He wanted to show that fate ruled people's lives, and that those who interfered with it did so to their sorrow.   He put a spell on it so that three separate men could each have three wishes from it."

His manner was so impressive that his hearers were conscious that their light laughter jarred somewhat.

"Well, why don't you have three, sir?" said Herbert White, cleverly.

The soldier regarded him in the way that middle age is wont to regard presumptuous youth. "I have," he said, quietly, and his blotchy face whitened.

"And did you really have the three wishes granted?" asked Mrs. White.

"I did," said the sergeant-major, and his glass tapped against his strong teeth.

"And has anybody else wished?" persisted the old lady.

"The first man had his three wishes. Yes," was the reply; "I don't know what the first two were, but the third was for death. That's how I got the paw."

His tones were so grave that a hush fell upon the group.

"If you've had your three wishes, it's no good to you now, then, Morris," said the old man at last. "What do you keep it for?"

The soldier shook his head. "Fancy, I suppose," he said, slowly. "I did have some idea of selling it, but I don't think I will. It has caused enough mischief already. Besides, people won't buy. They think it's a fairy tale; some of them, and those who do think anything of it want to try it first and pay me afterward."

"If you could have another three wishes," said the old man, eyeing him keenly, "would you have them?"

"I don't know," said the other. "I don't know."

He took the paw, and dangling it between

his forefinger and thumb, suddenly threw it upon the fire. White, with a slight cry, stooped down and snatched it off.

"Better let it burn," said the soldier, solemnly.

"If you don't want it, Morris," said the other, "give it to me."

"I won't," said his friend, doggedly. "I threw it on the fire. If you keep it, don't blame me for what happens. Pitch it on the fire again like a sensible man."

The other shook his head and examined his new possession closely. "How do you do it?" he inquired.

"Hold it up in your right hand and wish aloud," said the sergeant-major, "but I warn you of the consequences."

"Sounds like the *Arabian Nights*," said Mrs. White, as she rose and began to set the supper. "Don't you think you might wish for four pairs of hands for me?"

Her husband drew the talisman from pocket, and then all three burst into laughter as the sergeant-major, with a look of alarm on his face, caught him by the arm.

"If you must wish," he said, gruffly, "wish for something sensible."

Mr. White dropped it back in his pocket, and placing chairs, motioned his friend to the table. In the business of supper the talisman was partly forgotten, and afterward the three sat listening in an enthralled fashion to a second instalment of the soldier's adventures in India.

"If the tale about the monkey's paw is not more truthful than those he has been telling us," said Herbert, as the door closed behind their guest, just in time for him to catch the last train, "we sha'nt make much out of it."

"Did you give him anything for it, father?" inquired Mrs. White, regarding her husband closely.

"A trifle," said he, colouring slightly. "He didn't want it, but I made him take it. And he pressed me again to throw it away."

"Likely," said Herbert, with pretended horror. "Why, we're going to be rich, and famous and happy. Wish to be an emperor, father, to begin with; then you can't be henpecked."

He darted round the table, pursued by the maligned Mrs. White armed with an antimacassar.

Mr. White took the paw from his pocket and eyed it dubiously. "I don't know what to wish for, and that's a fact," he said, slowly. "It seems to me I've got all I want."

"If you only cleared the house, you'd be quite happy, wouldn't you?" said Herbert, with his hand on his shoulder. "Well, wish for two hundred pounds, then; that 'll just do it."

His father, smiling shamefacedly at his own credulity, held up the talisman, as his son, with a solemn face, somewhat marred by a wink at his mother, sat down at the piano and struck a few impressive chords.

"I wish for two hundred pounds," said the old man distinctly.

A fine crash from the piano greeted the words, interrupted by a shuddering cry from the old man. His wife and son ran toward him.

"It moved," he cried, with a glance of disgust at the object as it lay on the floor.

"As I wished, it twisted in my hand like a snake."

"Well, I don't see the money," said his son as he picked it up and placed it on the table, "and I bet I never shall."

"It must have been your fancy, father," said his wife, regarding him anxiously.

He shook his head. "Never mind, though; there's no harm done, but it gave me a shock all the same."

They sat down by the fire again while the two men finished their pipes. Outside, the wind was higher than ever, and the old man started nervously at the sound of a door banging upstairs. A silence unusual and depressing settled upon all three, which lasted until the old couple rose to retire for the night.

"I expect you'll find the cash tied up in a big bag in the middle of your bed," said Herbert, as he bade them good-night, "and something horrible squatting up on top of the wardrobe watching you as you pocket your ill-gotten gains."

He sat alone in the darkness, gazing at the dying fire, and seeing faces in it. The last face was so horrible and so simian that he gazed at it in amazement. It got so vivid that, with a little uneasy laugh, he felt on the table for a glass containing a little water to throw over it. His hand grasped the monkey's paw, and with a little shiver he wiped his hand on his coat and went up to bed.

II.

In the brightness of the wintry sun next morning as it streamed over the breakfast table he laughed at his fears. There was an air of prosaic wholesomeness about the room which it had lacked on the previous night, and the dirty, shrivelled little paw was pitched on the sideboard with a carelessness which betokened no great belief in its virtues.

"I suppose all old soldiers are the same," said Mrs. White. "The idea of our listening to such nonsense! How could wishes be granted in these days? And if they could, how could two hundred pounds hurt you, father?"

"Might drop on his head from the sky," said the frivolous Herbert.

"Morris said the things happened so naturally," said his father, "that you might if you so wished attribute it to coincidence."

"Well, don't break into the money before I come back," said Herbert as he rose from the table. "I'm afraid it'll turn you into a mean, avaricious man, and we shall have to disown you."

His mother laughed, and following him to the door, watched him down the road; and returning to the breakfast table, was very happy at the expense of her husband's credulity. All of which did not prevent her from scurrying to the door at the postman's knock, nor prevent her from referring somewhat shortly to retired sergeant-majors of bibulous habits when she found that the post brought a tailor's bill.

"Herbert will have some more of his funny remarks, I expect, when he comes home," she said, as they sat at dinner.

"I dare say," said Mr. White, pouring himself out some beer; "but for all that, the thing moved in my hand; that I'll swear to."

"You thought it did," said the old lady soothingly.

"I say it did," replied the other. "There was no thought about it; I had just——— What's the matter?"

His wife made no reply. She was watching the mysterious movements of a man outside, who, peering in an undecided fashion at the house, appeared to be trying to make up his mind to enter. In mental connection with the two hundred pounds, she noticed that the stranger was well dressed, and wore a silk hat of glossy newness. Three times he paused at the gate, and then walked on again. The fourth time he stood with his hand upon it, and then with sudden resolution flung it open and walked up the path. Mrs. White at the same moment placed her hands behind her, and hurriedly unfastening the strings of her apron, put that useful article of apparel beneath the cushion of her chair.

She brought the stranger, who seemed ill at ease, into the room. He gazed at her furtively, and listened in a preoccupied fashion as the old lady apologized for the appearance of the room, and her husband's coat, a garment which he usually reserved for the garden. She then waited as patiently as her sex would permit, for him to broach his business, but he was at first strangely silent.

"I—was asked to call," he said at last, and stooped and picked a piece of cotton from his trousers. "I come from 'Maw and Meggins.'"

The old lady started. "Is anything the matter?" she asked, breathlessly. "Has anything happened to Herbert? What is it? What is it?"

Her husband interposed. "There, there, mother," he said, hastily. "Sit down, and don't jump to conclusions. You've not brought bad news, I'm sure, sir;" and he eyed the other wistfully.

"I'm sorry—" began the visitor.

"Is he hurt?" demanded the mother, wildly.

The visitor bowed in assent. "Badly hurt," he said, quietly, "but he is not in any pain."

"Oh, thank God!" said the old woman, clasping her hands. "Thank God for that! Thank——"

She broke off suddenly as the sinister meaning of the assurance dawned upon her and she saw the awful confirmation of her fears in the other's perverted face. She caught her breath, and turning to her slower-witted husband, laid her trembling old hand upon his. There was a long silence.

"He was caught in the machinery," said the visitor at length in a low voice.

"Caught in the machinery," repeated Mr. White, in a dazed fashion, "yes."

He sat staring blankly out at the window, and taking his wife's hand between his own, pressed it as he had been wont to do in their old courting-days nearly forty years before.

"He was the only one left to us," he said, turning gently to the visitor.   "It is hard."

The other coughed, and rising, walked slowly to the window.   "The firm wished me to convey their sincere sympathy with you in your great loss," he said, without looking round.   "I beg that you will understand I am only their servant and merely obeying orders."

There was no reply; the old woman's face was white, her eyes staring, and her breath inaudible; on the husband's face was a look such as his friend the sergeant might have carried into his first action.

"I was to say that Maw and Meggins disclaim all responsibility," continued the other. "They admit no liability at all, but in consideration of your son's services, they wish to present you with a certain sum as compensation."

Mr. White dropped his wife's hand, and rising to his feet, gazed with a look of horror at his visitor. His dry lips shaped the words, "How much?"

"Two hundred pounds," was the answer.

Unconscious of his wife's shriek, the old man smiled faintly, put out his hands like a sightless man, and dropped, a senseless heap, to the floor.

III.

IN the huge new cemetery, some two miles distant, the old people buried their dead, and came back to a house steeped in shadow and silence. It was all over so quickly that at first they could hardly realize it, and remained in a state of expectation as though of something else to happen—something else which was to lighten this load, too heavy for old hearts to bear.

But the days passed, and expectation gave place to resignation—the hopeless resignation of the old, sometimes miscalled, apathy. Sometimes they hardly exchanged a word, for now they had nothing to talk about, and their days were long to weariness.

It was about a week after that the old man, waking suddenly in the night, stretched out his hand and found himself alone. The room was in darkness, and the sound of subdued weeping came from the window.   He raised himself in bed and listened.

"Come back," he said, tenderly.   "You will be cold."

"It is colder for my son," said the old woman, and wept afresh.

The sound of her sobs died away on his ears.   The bed was warm, and his eyes heavy with sleep.   He dozed fitfully, and then slept until a sudden wild cry from his wife awoke him with a start.

"*The paw!*" she cried wildly.   "The monkey's paw!"

He started up in alarm.   "Where?   Where is it?   What's the matter?"

She came stumbling across the room toward him.   "I want it," she said, quietly.   "You've not destroyed it?"

"It's in the parlour, on the bracket," he replied, marvelling.   "Why?"

She cried and laughed together, and bending over, kissed his cheek.

"I only just thought of it," she said, hysterically.   "Why didn't I think of it before?   Why didn't *you* think of it?"

"Think of what?" he questioned.

"The other two wishes," she replied, rapidly. "We've only had one."

"Was not that enough?" he demanded, fiercely.

"No," she cried, triumphantly; "we'll have one more. Go down and get it quickly, and wish our boy alive again."

The man sat up in bed and flung the bedclothes from his quaking limbs. "Good God, you are mad!" he cried, aghast.

"Get it," she panted; "get it quickly, and wish—— Oh, my boy, my boy!"

Her husband struck a match and lit the candle. "Get back to bed," he said, unsteadily. "You don't know what you are saying."

"We had the first wish granted," said the old woman, feverishly; "why not the second?"

"A coincidence," stammered the old man.

"Go and get it and wish," cried his wife, quivering with excitement.

The old man turned and regarded her, and his voice shook. "He has been dead ten days, and besides he—I would not tell you else, but—I could only recognize him by his clothing. If he was too terrible for you to see then, how now?"

"Bring him back," cried the old woman, and dragged him toward the door. "Do you think I fear the child I have nursed?"

He went down in the darkness, and felt his way to the parlour, and then to the mantel-piece. The talisman was in its place, and a horrible fear that the unspoken wish might bring his mutilated son before him ere he could escape from the room seized upon him, and he caught his breath as he found that he had lost the direction of the door. His brow cold with sweat, he felt his way round the table, and groped along the wall until he found himself in the small passage with the unwholesome thing in his hand.

Even his wife's face seemed changed as he entered the room. It was white and expectant, and to his fears seemed to have an unnatural look upon it. He was afraid of her.

"*Wish!*" she cried, in a strong voice.

"It is foolish and wicked," he faltered.

"*Wish!*" repeated his wife.

He raised his hand. "I wish my son alive again."

The talisman fell to the floor, and he regarded it fearfully. Then he sank trembling into a chair as the old woman, with burning eyes, walked to the window and raised the blind.

He sat until he was chilled with the cold, glancing occasionally at the figure of the old woman peering through the window. The candle-end, which had burned below the rim of the china candlestick, was throwing pulsating shadows on the ceiling and walls, until, with a flicker larger than the rest, it expired. The old man, with an unspeakable sense of relief at the failure of the talisman, crept back to his bed, and a minute or two afterward the old woman came silently and apathetically beside him.

Neither spoke, but lay silently listening to the ticking of the clock. A stair creaked, and a squeaky mouse scurried noisily through the wall. The darkness was oppressive, and after lying for some time screwing up his courage, he took the box of matches, and striking one, went downstairs for a candle.

At the foot of the stairs the match went out,

"WHAT'S THAT?" CRIED THE OLD WOMAN.

and he paused to strike another; and at the same moment a knock, so quiet and stealthy as to be scarcely audible, sounded on the front door.

The matches fell from his hand and spilled in the passage. He stood motionless, his breath suspended until the knock was repeated. Then he turned and fled swiftly back to his room, and closed the door behind him. A third knock sounded through the house.

"What's that?" cried the old woman, starting up.

"A rat," said the old man in shaking tones— "a rat. It passed me on the stairs."

His wife sat up in bed listening. A loud knock resounded through the house.

"It's Herbert!" she screamed. "It's Herbert!"

She ran to the door, but her husband was before her, and catching her by the arm, held her tightly.

"What are you going to do?" he whispered hoarsely.

"It's my boy; it's Herbert!" she cried, struggling mechanically. "I forgot it was two miles away. What are you holding me for? Let go. I must open the door.

"For God's sake don't let it in," cried the old man, trembling.

"You're afraid of your own son," she cried, struggling. "Let me go. I'm coming, Herbert; I'm coming."

There was another knock, and another. The old woman with a sudden wrench broke free and ran from the room. Her husband followed to the landing, and called after her appealingly as she hurried downstairs. He heard the chain rattle back and the bottom bolt drawn slowly and stiffly from the socket. Then the old woman's voice, strained and panting.

"The bolt," she cried, loudly. "Come down. I can't reach it."

But her husband was on his hands and knees groping wildly on the floor in search of the paw. If he could only find it before the thing outside got in. A perfect fusillade of knocks reverberated through the house, and he heard the scraping of a chair as his wife put it down in the passage against the door. He heard the creaking of the bolt as it came slowly back, and at the same moment he found the monkey's paw, and frantically breathed his third and last wish.

The knocking ceased suddenly, although the echoes of it were still in the house. He heard the chair drawn back, and the door opened. A cold wind rushed up the staircase, and a long loud wail of disappointment and misery from his wife gave him courage to run down to her side, and then to the gate beyond. The street lamp flickering opposite shone on a quiet and deserted road.

Bill's Paper Chase

BILL'S PAPER CHASE

SAILORMEN 'ave their faults, said the night watchman, frankly. I'm not denying of it. I used to 'ave myself when I was at sea, but being close with their money is a fault as can seldom be brought ag'in 'em.

I saved some money once—two golden sovereigns, owing to a 'ole in my pocket. Before I got another ship I slept two nights on a doorstep and 'ad nothing to eat, and I found them two sovereigns in the lining o' my coat when I was over two thousand miles away from the nearest pub.

I on'y knew one miser all the years I was at sea. Thomas Geary 'is name was, and we was shipmates aboard the barque *Grenada,* homeward bound from Sydney to London.

Thomas was a man that was getting into years; sixty, I think 'e was, and old enough to know better. 'E'd been saving 'ard for over forty years, and as near as we could make out 'e was worth a matter o' six 'undered pounds. He used to be fond o' talking about it, and letting us know how much better off 'e was than any of the rest of us.

We was about a month out from Sydney when old Thomas took sick. Bill Hicks said that it was owing to a ha'penny he couldn't account for; but Walter Jones, whose family was always ill, and thought 'e knew a lot about it, said that 'e knew wot it was, but 'e couldn't remember the name of it, and that when we got to London and Thomas saw a doctor, we should see as 'ow 'e was right.

Whatever it was the old man got worse and worse. The skipper came down and gave 'im some physic and looked at 'is tongue, and then 'e looked at our tongues to see wot the difference was. Then 'e left the cook in charge of 'im and went off.

The next day Thomas was worse, and it was soon clear to everybody but 'im that 'e was slipping 'is cable. He wouldn't believe it at first, though the cook told 'im, Bill Hicks told him, and Walter Jones 'ad a grandfather that went off in just the same way.

"I'm not going to die," says Thomas "How can I die and leave all that money?"

"It'll be good for your relations, Thomas," says Walter Jones.

"I ain't got any," says the old man.

"Well, your friends, then, Thomas," says Walter, soft-like.

"Ain't got any," says the old man ag'in.

"Yes, you 'ave, Thomas," says Walter, with a kind smile; "I could tell you one you've got."

Thomas shut his eyes at 'im and began to talk pitiful about 'is money and the 'ard work 'e'd 'ad saving of it. And by-and-by 'e got worse, and didn't reckernise us, but thought we was a pack o' greedy, drunken sailormen. He thought Walter Jones was a shark, and told 'im so, and, try all 'e could, Walter couldn't persuade 'im different.

He died the day arter. In the morning 'e was whimpering about 'is money ag'in, and angry with Bill when 'e reminded 'im that 'e couldn't take it with 'im, and 'e made Bill promise that 'e should be buried just as 'e was. Bill tucked him up arter that, and when 'e felt a canvas belt tied round the old man's waist 'e began to see wot 'e was driving at.

The weather was dirty that day and there was a bit o' sea running, consequently all 'ands was on deck, and a boy about sixteen wot used to 'elp the steward down aft was lookin' arter Thomas. Me and Bill just run down to give a look at the old man in time.

"I *am* going to take it with me, Bill," says the old man.

"That's right," says Bill.

"My mind's—easy now," says Thomas. "I gave it to Jimmy—to—to—throw overboard for me."

"*Wot?*" says Bill, staring.

"That's right, Bill," says the boy. "He told me to. It was a little packet o' banknotes. He gave me tuppence for doing it."

Old Thomas seemed to be listening. 'Is eyes was open, and 'e looked artful at Bill to think what a clever thing 'e'd done.

"Nobody's goin'—to spend—*my* money," 'e says. "Nobody's——"

We drew back from 'is bunk and stood staring at 'im. Then Bill turned to the boy.

"Go and tell the skipper 'e's gone," 'e says, "and mind, for your own sake, don't tell the skipper or anybody else that you've thrown all that money overboard."

"Why not?" says Jimmy.

"Becos you'll be locked up for it," says Bill; "you'd no business to do it. You've been and broke the law. It ought to ha' been left to somebody."

Jimmy looked scared, and arter 'e was gone I turned to Bill, and I looks at 'im and I says: "What's the little game, Bill?"

"*Game?*" said Bill, snorting at me. "I don't want the pore boy to get into trouble, do I? Pore little chap. You was young yourself once."

"Yes," I says; "but I'm a bit older now, Bill, and unless you tell me what your little game is, I shall tell the skipper myself, and the chaps too. Pore old Thomas told 'im to do it, so where's the boy to blame?"

"Do you think Jimmy *did?*" says Bill, screwing up his nose at me. "That little varmint is walking about worth six 'undered quid.

Now you keep your mouth shut and I'll make it worth your while."

Then I see Bill's game. "All right, I'll keep quiet for the sake of my half," I says, looking at 'im.

I thought he'd ha' choked, and the langwidge 'e see fit to use was a'most as much as I could answer.

"Very well, then," 'e says, at last, "halves it is. It ain't robbery becos it belongs to nobody, and it ain't the boy's becos 'e was told to throw it overboard."

They buried pore old Thomas next morning, and arter it was all over Bill put 'is 'and on the boy's shoulder as they walked for'ard and 'e says, "Poor old Thomas 'as gone to look for 'is money," he says; "wonder whether 'e'll find it! Was it a big bundle, Jimmy?"

"No," says the boy, shaking 'is 'ead. "They was six 'undered pound notes and two sovereigns, and I wrapped the sovereigns up in the notes to make 'em sink. Fancy throwing money away like that, Bill: seems a sin, don't it?"

Bill didn't answer 'im, and that afternoon the other chaps below being asleep we searched 'is bunk through and through without any luck, and at last Bill sat down and swore 'e must ha' got it about 'im.

We waited till night, and when everybody was snoring 'ard we went over to the boy's bunk and went all through 'is pockets and felt the linings, and then we went back to our side and Bill said wot 'e thought about Jimmy in whispers.

"He must ha' got it tied round 'is waist next to 'is skin, like Thomas 'ad," I says.

We stood there in the dark whispering, and then Bill couldn't stand it any longer, and 'e went over on tiptoe to the bunk ag'in. He was tremblin' with excitement and I wasn't much better, when all of a sudden the cook sat up in 'is bunk with a dreadful laughing scream and called out that somebody was ticklin' 'im.

I got into my bunk and Bill got into 'is, and we lay there listening while the cook, who was a terrible ticklish man, leaned out of 'is bunk and said wot 'e'd do if it 'appened ag'in.

"Go to sleep," says Walter Jones; "you're

dreamin'. Who d'you think would want to tickle you?"

"I tell you," says the cook, "somebody come over and tickled me with a 'and the size of a leg o' mutton. I feel creepy all over."

Bill gave it up for that night, but the next day 'e pretended to think Jimmy was gettin' fat an' 'e caught 'old of 'im and prodded 'im all over. He thought 'e felt something round 'is waist, but 'e couldn't be sure, and Jimmy made such a noise that the other chaps interfered and told Bill to leave 'im alone.

For a whole week we tried to find that money, and couldn't, and Bill said it was a suspicious thing that Jimmy kept aft a good deal more than 'e used to, and 'e got an idea that the boy might ha' 'idden it somewhere there. At the end of that time, 'owever, owing to our being short-'anded, Jimmy was sent for'ard to work as ordinary seaman, and it began to be quite noticeable the way 'e avoided Bill.

At last one day we got 'im alone down the fo'c'sle, and Bill put 'is arm round 'im and got 'im on the locker and asked 'im straight out where the money was.

"Why, I chucked it overboard," he says.   "I told you so afore.   What a memory you've got, Bill!"

Bill picked 'im up and laid 'im on the locker, and we searched 'im thoroughly.   We even took 'is boots off, and then we 'ad another look in 'is bunk while 'e was putting 'em on ag'in.

"If you're innercent," says Bill, "why don't you call out?—eh?"

"Because you told me not to say anything about it, Bill," says the boy.   "But I will next time.   Loud, I will."

"Look 'ere," says Bill, "you tell us where it is, and the three of us'll go shares in it.   That'll be two 'undered pounds each, and we'll tell you 'ow to get yours changed without getting caught.   We're cleverer than you are, you know."

"I know that, Bill," says the boy; "but it's no good me telling you lies.   I chucked it overboard."

"Very good, then," says Bill, getting up. "I'm going to tell the skipper."

"Tell 'im," says Jimmy.   "I don't care."

"Then you'll be searched *arter you've stepped ashore*," says Bill, "and you won't be allowed on the ship ag'in.   You'll lose it all by being greedy, whereas if you go shares with us you'll 'ave two 'undered pounds."

I could see as 'ow the boy 'adn't thought o' that, and try as 'e would 'e couldn't 'ide 'is feelin's.   He called Bill a red-nosed shark, and 'e called me somethin' I've forgotten now.

"Think it over," says Bill; "mind, you'll be collared as soon as you've left the gangway and searched by the police."

"And will they tickle the cook too, I wonder?" says Jimmy, savagely.

"And if they find it you'll go to prison," says Bill, giving 'im a clump o' the side o' the 'ead, "and you won't like that, I can tell you."

"Why, ain't it nice, Bill?" says Jimmy, holding 'is ear.

Bill looked at 'im and then 'e steps to the ladder.   "I'm not going to talk to you any more, my lad," 'e says.   "I'm going to tell the skipper."

He went up slowly, and just as 'e reached the deck Jimmy started up and called 'im.   Bill pretended not to 'ear, and the boy ran up on deck and follered 'im; and arter a little while they both came down again together.

"Did you wish to speak to me, my lad?" says Bill, 'olding 'is 'ead up.

"Yes," says the boy, fiddling with 'is fingers; "if you keep your ugly mouth shut, we'll go shares."

"Ho!" says Bill, "I thought you throwed it overboard!"

"I thought so, too, Bill," says Jimmy, very softly, "and when I came below ag'in I found it in my trousers pocket."

"Where is it now?" says Bill.

"Never mind where it is," says the boy; "you couldn't get it if I was to tell you. It'll take me all my time to do it myself."

"Where is it?" says Bill, ag'in. "I'm goin' to take care of it. I won't trust you."

"And I can't trust you," says Jimmy.

"If you don't tell me where it is this minute," says Bill, moving to the ladder ag'in, "I'm off to tell the skipper. I want it in my 'ands, or at any rate my share of it. Why not share it out now?"

"Because I 'aven't got it," says Jimmy, stamping 'is foot, "that's why, and it's all your silly fault. Arter you came pawing through my pockets when you thought I was asleep I got frightened and 'id it."

"Where?" says Bill.

"In the second mate's mattress," says Jimmy. "I was tidying up down aft and I found a 'ole in the underneath side of 'is mattress and I shoved it in there, and poked it in with a bit o' stick."

"And 'ow are you going to get it?" says Bill, scratching 'is 'ead.

"That's wot I don't know, seeing that I'm not allowed aft now," says Jimmy. "One of us'll 'ave to make a dash for it when we get to London. And mind if there's any 'anky-panky on your part, Bill, I'll give the show away myself."

The cook came down just then and we 'ad to leave off talking, and I could see that Bill was so pleased at finding that the money 'adn't been thrown overboard that 'e was losing sight o' the difficulty o' getting at it. In a day or two, 'owever, 'e see it as plain as me and Jimmy did, and, as time went by, he got desprit, and frightened us both by 'anging about aft every chance 'e got.

The companion-way faced the wheel, and there was about as much chance o' getting down there without being seen as there would be o' taking a man's false teeth out of 'is mouth without 'is knowing it. Jimmy went down one day while Bill was at the wheel to look for 'is knife, wot 'e thought 'e'd left down there, and 'ed 'ardly got down afore Bill saw 'im come up ag'in, 'olding on to the top of a mop which the steward was using.

We couldn't figure it out nohow, and to think o' the second mate, a little man with a large fam'ly, who never 'ad a penny in 'is pocket, sleeping every night on a six 'undered pound mattress, sent us pretty near crazy. We used to talk it over whenever we got a chance, and Bill and Jimmy could scarcely be civil to each other. The boy said it was Bill's fault, and 'e said it was the boy's.

"The on'y thing I can see," says the boy, one day, "is for Bill to 'ave a touch of sunstroke as 'e's leaving the wheel one day, tumble 'ead-first

down the companion-way, and injure 'isself so
severely that 'e can't be moved. Then they'll
put 'im in a cabin down aft, and p'raps I'll 'ave
to go and nurse 'im. Anyway, *he'll* be down
there."

"It's a very good idea, Bill," I says.

"Ho," says Bill, looking at me as if 'e would
eat me. "Why don't you do it, then?"

"I'd sooner you did it, Bill," says the boy;
"still, I don't mind which it is. Why not toss
up for it?"

"Get away," says Bill. "Get away afore I
do something you won't like, you blood-thirsty
little murderer."

"I've got a plan myself," he says, in a low
voice, after the boy 'ad 'opped off, "and if I
can't think of nothing better I'll try it, and
mind, not a word to the boy."

He didn't think o' nothing better, and one
night just as we was making the Channel 'e
tried 'is plan. He was in the second mate's
watch, and by-and-by 'e leans over the wheel
and says to 'im in a low voice, "This is my last
v'y'ge, sir."

"Oh," says the second mate, who was a man

as didn't mind talking to a man before the mast.
"How's that?"

"I've got a berth ashore, sir," says Bill, "and
I wanted to ask a favour, sir."

The second mate growled and walked off
a pace or two.

"I've never been so 'appy as I've been on this
ship," says Bill; "none of us 'ave. We was
saying so the other night, and everybody
agreed as it was owing to you, sir, and your
kindness to all of us."

The second mate coughed, but Bill could see
as 'e was a bit pleased.

"The feeling came over me," says Bill, "that
when I leave the sea for good I'd like to 'ave
something o' yours to remember you by, sir.
And it seemed to me that if I 'ad your mattress
I should think of you ev'ry night o' my life."

"My *wot?*" says the second mate, staring at
'im.

"Your mattress, sir," says Bill. "If I might
make so bold as to offer a pound for it, sir. I
want something wot's been used by you, and
I've got a fancy for that as a keepsake."

The second mate shook 'is 'ead. "I'm

sorry, Bill," 'e says, gently, "but I couldn't let it go at that."

"I'd sooner pay thirty shillin's than not 'ave it, sir," says Bill, 'umbly.

"I gave a lot of money for that mattress," says the mate, ag'in. "I forgit 'ow much, but a lot. You don't know 'ow valuable that mattress is."

"I know it's a good one, sir, else you wouldn't 'ave it," says Bill. "Would a couple o' pounds buy it, sir?"

The second mate hum'd and ha'd, but Bill was afeard to go any 'igher. So far as 'e could make out from Jimmy, the mattress was worth about eighteen pence—to anybody who wasn't pertiklar.

"I've slept on that mattress for years," says the second mate, looking at 'im from the corner of 'is eye. "I don't believe I could sleep on another. Still, to oblige you, Bill, you shall 'ave it at that if you don't want it till we go ashore?"

"Thankee, sir," says Bill, 'ardly able to keep from dancing, "and I'll 'and over the two pounds when we're paid off. I shall keep it all

my life, sir, in memory of you and your kindness."

"And mind you keep quiet about it," says
the second mate, who didn't want the skipper
to know wot 'e'd been doing, "because I don't
want to be bothered by other men wanting to
buy things as keepsakes."

Bill promised 'im like a shot, and when 'e
told me about it 'e was nearly crying with joy.

"And mind," 'e says, "I've bought that mattress, bought it as it stands, and it's got nothing
to do with Jimmy. We'll each pay a pound
and halve wot's in it."

He persuaded me at last, but that boy
watched us like a cat watching a couple of can-
aries, and I could see we should 'ave all we
could do to deceive *'im*. He seemed more suspicious o' Bill than me, and 'e kep' worrying
us nearly every day to know what we were going to do.

We beat about in the channel with a strong
'ead-wind for four days, and then a tug picked
us up and towed us to London.

The excitement of that last little bit was
'orrible. Fust of all we 'ad got to get the mat-

tress, and then in some way we 'ad got to get rid o' Jimmy.   Bill's idea was for me to take 'im ashore with me and tell 'im that Bill would join us arterwards, and then lose 'im; but I said that till I'd got my share I couldn't bear to lose sight o' Bill's honest face for 'alf a second.

And, besides, Jimmy wouldn't 'ave gone. All the way up the river 'e stuck to Bill, and kept asking 'im wot we were to do. 'E was 'alf crying, and so excited that Bill was afraid the other chaps would notice it.

We got to our berth in the East India Docks at last, and arter we were made fast we went below to 'ave a wash and change into our shore-going togs.   Jimmy watched us all the time, and then 'e comes up to Bill biting 'is nails, and says:

"How's it to be done, Bill?"

"Hang about arter the rest 'ave gone ashore, and trust to luck," says Bill, looking at me. "We'll see 'ow the land lays when we draw our advance."

We went down aft to draw ten shillings each to go ashore with.   Bill and me got ours fust, and then the second mate who 'ad tipped 'im the wink followed us out unconcerned-like and 'anded Bill the mattress rolled up in a sack.

"'Ere you are, Bill," 'e says.

"Much obliged, sir," says Bill, and 'is 'ands trembled so as 'e could 'ardly 'old it, and 'e made to go off afore Jimmy come on deck.

Then that fool of a mate kept us there while 'e made a little speech. Twice Bill made to go off, but 'e put 'is 'and on 'is arm and kept 'im there while 'e told 'im 'ow he'd always tried to be liked by the men, and 'ad generally suc-ceeded, and in the middle of it up popped Mas-ter Jimmy.

He gave a start as he saw the bag, and 'is eyes opened wide, and then as we walked for-'ard 'e put 'is arm through Bill's and called 'im all the names 'e could think of.

"You'd steal the milk out of a cat's saucer," 'e says; "but mind, you don't leave this ship till I've got my share."

"I meant it for a pleasant surprise for you, Jimmy," says Bill, trying to smile.

"I don't like your surprises, Bill, so I don't deceive you," says the boy.   "Where are you going to open it?"

"I was thinking of opening it in my bunk," says Bill.   "The perlice might want to examine it if we took it through the dock.   Come on, Jimmy, old man."

"Yes; all right," says the boy, nodding 'is 'ead at 'im.   "I'll stay up 'ere.   You might forget yourself, Bill, if I trusted myself down there with you alone.   You can throw my share up to me, and then you'll leave the ship afore I do.   See?"

"Go to blazes," says Bill; and then, seeing that the last chance 'ad gone, we went below, and 'e chucked the bundle in 'is bunk.   There was only one chap down there, and arter spending best part o' ten minutes doing 'is hair 'e nodded to us and went off.

Half a minute later Bill cut open the mattress and began to search through the stuffing, while I struck matches and watched 'im.   It wasn't a big mattress and there wasn't much stuffing, but we couldn't seem to see that money.   Bill went all over it ag'in and ag'in, and then 'e stood up and looked at me and caught 'is breath painful.

"Do you think the mate found it?" 'e says, in a 'usky voice.

We went through it ag'in, and then Bill went half-way up the fo'c's'le ladder and called soft-ly for Jimmy.   He called three times, and then, with a sinking sensation in 'is stummick, 'e went up on deck and I follered 'im.   The boy was nowhere to be seen.   All we saw was the ship's cat 'aving a wash and brush-up afore going ashore, and the skipper standing aft talk-ing to the owner.

We never saw that boy ag'in.   He never turned up for 'is box, and 'e didn't show up to draw 'is pay.   Everybody else was there, of course, and arter I'd got mine and come out-side I see pore Bill with 'is back up ag'in a wall, staring 'ard at the second mate, who was look-ing at 'im with a kind smile, and asking 'im 'ow he'd slept.   The last thing I saw of Bill, the pore chap 'ad got 'is 'ands in 'is trousers pockets, and was trying 'is hardest to smile back.

The Well

THE WELL

Two men stood in the billiard-room of an old country house, talking. Play, which had been of a half-hearted nature, was over, and they sat at the open window, looking out over the park stretching away beneath them, conversing idly.

"Your time's nearly up, Jem," said one at length, "this time six weeks you'll be yawning out the honeymoon and cursing the man—woman I mean—who invented them."

Jem Benson stretched his long limbs in the chair and grunted in dissent.

"I've never understood it," continued Wilfred Carr, yawning. "It's not in my line at all; I never had enough money for my own wants, let alone for two. Perhaps if I were as rich as you or Crœsus I might regard it differently."

There was just sufficient meaning in the latter part of the remark for his cousin to forbear to reply to it. He continued to gaze out of the window and to smoke slowly.

"Not being as rich as Crœsus—or you," resumed Carr, regarding him from beneath lowered lids, "I paddle my own canoe down the stream of Time, and, tying it to my friends' door-posts, go in to eat their dinners."

"Quite Venetian," said Jem Benson, still looking out of the window. "It's not a bad thing for you, Wilfred, that you have the door-posts and dinners—and friends."

Carr grunted in his turn. "Seriously though, Jem," he said, slowly, "you're a lucky fellow, a very lucky fellow. If there is a better girl above ground than Olive, I should like to see her."

"Yes," said the other, quietly.

"She's such an exceptional girl," continued Carr staring out of the window. "She's so good and gentle. She thinks you are a bundle of all the virtues."

He laughed frankly and joyously, but the other man did not join him.

"Strong sense of right and wrong, though,"

continued Carr, musingly. "Do you know, I believe that if she found out that you were not——"

"Not what?" demanded Benson, turning upon him fiercely, "Not what?"

"Everything that you are," returned his cousin, with a grin that belied his words, "I believe she'd drop you."

"Talk about something else," said Benson, slowly; "your pleasantries are not always in the best taste."

Wilfred Carr rose and taking a cue from the rack, bent over the board and practiced one or two favourite shots. "The only other subject I can talk about just at present is my own financial affairs," he said slowly, as he walked round the table.

"Talk about something else," said Benson again, bluntly.

"And the two things are connected," said Carr, and dropping his cue he half sat on the table and eyed his cousin.

There was a long silence. Benson pitched the end of his cigar out of the window, and leaning back closed his eyes.

"Do you follow me?" inquired Carr at length.

Benson opened his eyes and nodded at the window.

"Do you want to follow my cigar?" he demanded.

"I should prefer to depart by the usual way for your sake," returned the other, unabashed. "If I left by the window all sorts of questions would be asked, and you know what a talkative chap I am."

"So long as you don't talk about my affairs," returned the other, restraining himself by an obvious effort, "you can talk yourself hoarse."

"I'm in a mess," said Carr, slowly, "a devil of a mess.   If I don't raise fifteen hundred by this day fortnight, I may be getting my board and lodging free."

"Would that be any change?" questioned Benson.

The quality would," retorted the other. "The address also would not be good.   Seriously, Jem, will you let me have the fifteen hundred?"

"No," said the other, simply.

Carr went white. "It's to save me from ruin," he said, thickly.

"I've helped you till I'm tired," said Benson, turning and regarding him, "and it is all to no good. If you've got into a mess, get out of it. You should not be so fond of giving autographs away."

"It's foolish, I admit," said Carr, deliberately. "I won't do so any more. By the way, I've got some to sell. You needn't sneer. They're not my own."

"Whose are they?" inquired the other.

"Yours."

Benson got up from his chair and crossed over to him. "What is this?" he asked, quietly. "Blackmail?"

"Call it what you like," said Carr. "I've got some letters for sale, price fifteen hundred. And I know a man who would buy them at that price for the mere chance of getting Olive from you. I'll give you first offer."

"If you have got any letters bearing my signature, you will be good enough to give them to me," said Benson, very slowly.

"They're mine," said Carr, lightly; "given

to me by the lady you wrote them to.   I must say that they are not all in the best possible taste."

His cousin reached forward suddenly, and catching him by the collar of his coat pinned him down on the table.

"Give me those letters," he breathed, sticking his face close to Carr's.

"They're not here," said Carr, struggling. I'm not a fool.   Let me go, or I'll raise the price."

The other man raised him from the table in his powerful hands, apparently with the intention of dashing his head against it.   Then suddenly his hold relaxed as an astonished-looking maid-servant entered the room with letters. Carr sat up hastily.

"That's how it was done," said Benson, for the girl's benefit as he took the letters.

"I don't wonder at the other man making him pay for it, then," said Carr, blandly.

"You will give me those letters?" said Benson, suggestively, as the girl left the room.

"At the price I mentioned, yes," said Carr; "but so sure as I am a living man, if you lay your clumsy hands on me again, I'll double it. Now, I'll leave you for a time while you think it over."

He took a cigar from the box and lighting it carefully quitted the room. His cousin waited until the door had closed behind him, and then turning to the window sat there in a fit of fury as silent as it was terrible.

The air was fresh and sweet from the park, heavy with the scent of new-mown grass. The fragrance of a cigar was now added to it, and glancing out he saw his cousin pacing slowly by. He rose and went to the door, and then, apparently altering his mind, he returned to the window and watched the figure of his cousin as it moved slowly away into the moonlight. Then he rose again, and, for a long time, the room was empty.

*   *   *   *   *   *

It was empty when Mrs. Benson came in some time later to say good-night to her son on her way to bed. She walked slowly round the table, and pausing at the window gazed from it in idle thought, until she saw the figure of her son advancing with rapid strides toward the house. He looked up at the window.

"Good-night," said she.

"Good-night," said Benson, in a deep voice.

"Where is Wilfred?"

"Oh, he has gone," said Benson.

"Gone?"

"We had a few words; he was wanting money again, and I gave him a piece of my mind. I don't think we shall see him again."

"Poor Wilfred!" sighed Mrs. Benson. "He is always in trouble of some sort. I hope that you were not too hard upon him."

"No more than he deserved," said her son, sternly. "Good night."

II.

THE well, which had long ago fallen into disuse, was almost hidden by the thick tangle of undergrowth which ran riot at that corner of the old park. It was partly covered by the shrunken half of a lid, above which a rusty windlass creaked in company with the music of the pines when the wind blew strongly. The full light of the sun never reached it, and the ground surrounding it was moist and green when other parts of the park were gaping with the heat.

Two people walking slowly round the park in the fragrant stillness of a summer evening strayed in the direction of the well.

"No use going through this wilderness, Olive," said Benson, pausing on the outskirts of the pines and eyeing with some disfavour the gloom beyond.

"Best part of the park," said the girl briskly; "you know it's my favourite spot."

"I know you're very fond of sitting on the coping," said the man slowly, "and I wish you wouldn't. One day you will lean back too far and fall in."

"And make the acquaintance of Truth," said Olive lightly. "Come along."

She ran from him and was lost in the shadow of the pines, the bracken crackling beneath her feet as she ran. Her companion followed slowly, and emerging from the gloom saw her poised daintily on the edge of the well with her feet hidden in the rank grass and nettles which surrounded it. She motioned her companion to take a seat by her side, and smiled softly as she felt a strong arm passed about her waist.

"I like this place," said she, breaking a long silence, "it is so dismal—so uncanny. Do you know I wouldn't dare to sit here alone, Jem. I should imagine that all sorts of dreadful things were hidden behind the bushes and trees, waiting to spring out on me. Ugh!"

"You'd better let me take you in," said her companion tenderly; "the well isn't always wholesome, especially in the hot weather. Let's make a move."

The girl gave an obstinate little shake, and settled herself more securely on her seat.

"Smoke your cigar in peace," she said quietly. "I am settled here for a quiet talk. Has anything been heard of Wilfred yet?"

"Nothing."

"Quite a dramatic disappearance, isn't it?" she continued. "Another scrape, I suppose, and another letter for you in the same old strain; 'Dear Jem, help me out.'"

Jem Benson blew a cloud of fragrant smoke into the air, and holding his cigar between his teeth brushed away the ash from his coat sleeves.

"I wonder what he would have done without you," said the girl, pressing his arm affectionately. "Gone under long ago, I suppose. When we are married, Jem, I shall presume upon the relationship to lecture him. He is very wild, but he has his good points, poor fellow."

"I never saw them," said Benson, with startling bitterness. "God knows I never saw them."

"He is nobody's enemy but his own," said the girl, startled by this outburst.

"You don't know much about him," said the other, sharply. "He was not above blackmail; not above ruining the life of a friend to do himself a benefit. A loafer, a cur, and a liar!"

The girl looked up at him soberly but timidly and took his arm without a word, and they both sat silent while evening deepened into night and the beams of the moon, filtering through the branches, surrounded them with a silver network. Her head sank upon his shoulder, till suddenly with a sharp cry she sprang to her feet.

"What was that?" she cried breathlessly.

"What was what?" demanded Benson, springing up and clutching her fast by the arm.

She caught her breath and tried to laugh. "You're hurting me, Jem."

His hold relaxed.

"What is the matter?" he asked gently. "What was it startled you?"

"I was startled," she said, slowly, putting

her hands on his shoulder. "I suppose the words I used just now are ringing in my ears, but I fancied that somebody behind us whispered '*Jem, help me out.*'"

"Fancy," repeated Benson, and his voice shook; "but these fancies are not good for you. You—are frightened—at the dark and the gloom of these trees. Let me take you back to the house."

"No, I'm not frightened," said the girl, reseating herself. "I should never be really frightened of anything when you were with me, Jem. I'm surprised at myself for being so silly."

The man made no reply but stood, a strong, dark figure, a yard or two from the well, as though waiting for her to join him.

"Come and sit down, sir," cried Olive, patting the brickwork with her small, white hand, "one would think that you did not like your company."

He obeyed slowly and took a seat by her side, drawing so hard at his cigar that the light of it shone upon his face at every breath. He passed his arm, firm and rigid as steel, behind her, with his hand resting on the brickwork beyond.

"Are you warm enough?" he asked tenderly, as she made a little movement.

"Pretty fair," she shivered; "one oughtn't to be cold at this time of the year, but there's a cold, damp air comes up from the well."

As she spoke a faint splash sounded from the depths below, and for the second time that evening, she sprang from the well with a little cry of dismay.

"What is it now?" he asked in a fearful voice. He stood by her side and gazed at the well, as though half expecting to see the cause of her alarm emerge from it.

"Oh, my bracelet," she cried in distress, "my poor mother's bracelet. I've dropped it down the well."

"Your bracelet!" repeated Benson, dully. "Your bracelet? The diamond one?"

"The one that was my mother's," said Olive. "Oh, we can get it back surely. We must have the water drained off."

"Your bracelet!" repeated Benson, stupidly.

"Jem," said the girl in terrified tones, "dear Jem, what is the matter?"

For the man she loved was standing regarding her with horror. The moon which touched it was not responsible for all the whiteness of the distorted face, and she shrank back in fear to the edge of the well. He saw her fear and by a mighty effort regained his composure and took her hand.

"Poor little girl," he murmured, "you frightened me. I was not looking when you cried, and I thought that you were slipping from my arms, down—down——"

His voice broke, and the girl throwing herself into his arms clung to him convulsively.

"There, there," said Benson, fondly, "don't cry, don't cry."

"To-morrow," said Olive, half-laughing, half-crying, "we will all come round the well with hook and line and fish for it. It will be quite a new sport."

"No, we must try some other way," said Benson. "You shall have it back."

"How?" asked the girl.

"You shall see," said Benson. "To-morrow

morning at latest you shall have it back.   Till then promise me that you will not mention your loss to anyone.   Promise."

"I promise," said Olive, wonderingly.   "But why not?"

"It is of great value, for one thing, and— But there—there are many reasons.   For one thing it is my duty to get it for you."

"Wouldn't you like to jump down for it?" she asked mischievously.   "Listen."

She stooped for a stone and dropped it down.

"Fancy being where that is now," she said, peering into the blackness; "fancy going round and round like a mouse in a pail, clutching at the slimy sides, with the water filling your mouth, and looking up to the little patch of sky above."

"You had better come in," said Benson, very quietly.   "You are developing a taste for the morbid and horrible."

The girl turned, and taking his arm walked slowly in the direction of the house; Mrs. Benson, who was sitting in the porch, rose to receive them.

"You   shouldn't   have   kept   her   out   so

long," she said chidingly. "Where have you been?"

"Sitting on the well," said Olive, smiling, "discussing our future."

"I don't believe that place is healthy," said Mrs. Benson, emphatically. "I really think it might be filled in, Jem."

"All right," said her son, slowly. "Pity it wasn't filled in long ago."

He took the chair vacated by his mother as she entered the house with Olive, and with his hands hanging limply over the sides sat in deep thought. After a time he rose, and going upstairs to a room which was set apart for sporting requisites selected a sea fishing line and some hooks and stole softly downstairs again. He walked swiftly across the park in the direction of the well, turning before he entered the shadow of the trees to look back at the lighted windows of the house. Then having arranged his line he sat on the edge of the well and cautiously lowered it.

He sat with his lips compressed, occasionally looking about him in a startled fashion, as though he half expected to see something peering at him from the belt of trees.   Time after time he lowered his line until at length in pulling it up he heard a little metallic tinkle against the side of the well.

He held his breath then, and forgetting his fears drew the line in inch by inch, so as not to lose its precious burden.   His pulse beat rapidly, and his eyes were bright.   As the line came slowly in he saw the catch hanging to the hook, and with a steady hand drew the last few feet in.   Then he saw that instead of the bracelet he had hooked a bunch of keys.

With a faint cry he shook them from the hook into the water below, and stood breathing heavily.   Not a sound broke the stillness of the night.   He walked up and down a bit and stretched his great muscles; then he came back to the well and resumed his task.

For an hour or more the line was lowered without result.   In his eagerness he forgot his fears, and with eyes bent down the well fished slowly and carefully.   Twice the hook became entangled in something, and was with difficulty released.   It caught a third time, and all his efforts failed to free it.   Then he dropped the line down the well, and with head bent walked toward the house.

He went first to the stables at the rear, and then retiring to his room for some time paced restlessly up and down.   Then without removing his clothes he flung himself upon the bed and fell into a troubled sleep.

III.

Long before anybody else was astir he arose and stole softly downstairs. The sunlight was stealing in at every crevice, and flashing in long streaks across the darkened rooms. The dining-room into which he looked struck chill and cheerless in the dark yellow light which came through the lowered blinds. He remembered that it had the same appearance when his father lay dead in the house; now, as then, everything seemed ghastly and unreal; the very chairs standing as their occupants had left them the night before seemed to be indulging in some dark communication of ideas.

Slowly and noiselessly he opened the hall door and passed into the fragrant air beyond. The sun was shining on the drenched grass and trees, and a slowly vanishing white mist rolled like smoke about the grounds. For a moment he stood, breathing deeply the sweet air of the morning, and then walked slowly in the direction of the stables.

The rusty creaking of a pump-handle and a spatter of water upon the red-tiled courtyard showed that somebody else was astir, and a few steps farther he beheld a brawny, sandy-haired man gasping wildly under severe self-infliction at the pump.

"Everything ready, George?" he asked quietly.

"Yes, sir," said the man, straightening up suddenly and touching his forehead. "Bob's just finishing the arrangements inside. It's a lovely morning for a dip. The water in that well must be just icy."

"Be as quick as you can," said Benson, impatiently.

"Very good, sir," said George, burnishing his face harshly with a very small towel which had been hanging over the top of the pump. "Hurry up, Bob."

In answer to his summons a man appeared at the door of the stable with a coil of stout rope over his arm and a large metal candlestick in his hand.

"Just to try the air, sir," said George, following his master's glance, "a well gets rather foul sometimes, but if a candle can live down it, a man can."

His master nodded, and the man, hastily pulling up the neck of his shirt and thrusting his arms into his coat, followed him as he led the way slowly to the well.

"Beg pardon, sir," said George, drawing up to his side, "but you are not looking over and above well this morning. If you'll let me go down I'd enjoy the bath."

"No, no," said Benson, peremptorily.

"You ain't fit to go down, sir," persisted his follower. "I've never seen you look so before. Now if——"

"Mind your business," said his master curtly.

George became silent and the three walked with swinging strides through the long wet grass to the well. Bob flung the rope on the ground and at a sign from his master handed him the candlestick.

"Here's the line for it, sir," said Bob, fumbling in his pockets.

Benson took it from him and slowly tied it to the candlestick. Then he placed it on the edge of the well, and striking a match, lit the candle and began slowly to lower it.

"Hold hard, sir," said George, quickly, laying his hand on his arm, "you must tilt it or the string'll burn through."

Even as he spoke the string parted and the candlestick fell into the water below.

Benson swore quietly.

"I'll soon get another," said George, starting up.

"Never mind, the well's all right," said Benson.

"It won't take a moment, sir," said the other over his shoulder.

"Are you master here, or am I?" said Benson hoarsely.

George came back slowly, a glance at his master's face stopping the protest upon his tongue, and he stood by watching him sulkily as he sat on the well and removed his outer garments. Both men watched him curiously, as having completed his preparations he stood grim and silent with his hands by his sides.

"I wish you'd let me go, sir," said George, plucking up courage to address him. "You ain't fit to go, you've got a chill or something. I shouldn't wonder it's the typhoid. They've got it in the village bad."

For a moment Benson looked at him angrily, then his gaze softened. "Not this time, George," he said, quietly. He took the looped end of the rope and placed it under his arms, and sitting down threw one leg over the side of the well.

"How are you going about it, sir?" queried George, laying hold of the rope and signing to Bob to do the same.

"I'll call out when I reach the water," said Benson; "then pay out three yards more quickly so that I can get to the bottom."

"Very good, sir," answered both.

Their master threw the other leg over the coping and sat motionless. His back was turned toward the men as he sat with head bent, looking down the shaft. He sat for so long that George became uneasy.

"All right, sir?" he inquired.

"Yes," said Benson, slowly. "If I tug at the rope, George, pull up at once. Lower away."

The rope passed steadily through their hands until a hollow cry from the darkness below and a faint splashing warned them that he had reached the water. They gave him three yards more and stood with relaxed grasp and strained ears, waiting.

"He's gone under," said Bob in a low voice.

The other nodded, and moistening his huge palms took a firmer grip of the rope.

Fully a minute passed, and the men began to exchange uneasy glances. Then a sudden tremendous jerk followed by a series of feebler ones nearly tore the rope from their grasp.

"Pull!" shouted George, placing one foot on the side and hauling desperately. "Pull! pull! He's stuck fast; he's not coming; P—U— LL!"

In response to their terrific exertions the rope came slowly in, inch by inch, until at length a violent splashing was heard, and at the same moment a scream of unutterable horror came echoing up the shaft.

"What a weight he is!" panted Bob. "He's stuck fast or something. Keep still, sir; for heaven's sake, keep still."

For the taut rope was being jerked violently by the struggles of the weight at the end of it. Both men with grunts and sighs hauled it in foot by foot.

"All right, sir," cried George, cheerfully.

He had one foot against the well, and was pulling manfully; the burden was nearing the top. A long pull and a strong pull, and the face of a dead man with mud in the eyes and nostrils came peering over the edge. Behind it was the ghastly face of his master; but this he saw too late, for with a great cry he let go his hold of the rope and stepped back. The suddenness overthrew his assistant, and the rope tore through his hands. There was a frightful splash.

"You fool!" stammered Bob, and ran to the well helplessly.

"Run!" cried George. "Run for another line."

He bent over the coping and called eagerly down as his assistant sped back to the stables shouting wildly. His voice re-echoed down the shaft, but all else was silence.

Cupboard Love

CUPBOARD LOVE

In the comfortable living-room at Negget's farm, half parlour and half kitchen, three people sat at tea in the waning light of a November afternoon. Conversation, which had been brisk, had languished somewhat, owing to Mrs. Negget glancing at frequent intervals toward the door, behind which she was convinced the servant was listening, and checking the finest periods and the most startling suggestions with a warning *'ssh!*

"Go on, uncle," she said, after one of these interruptions.

"I forget where I was," said Mr. Martin Bodfish, shortly.

"Under our bed," Mr. Negget reminded him.

"Yes, watching," said Mrs. Negget, eagerly.

It was an odd place for an ex-policeman, especially as a small legacy added to his pension had considerably improved his social position, but Mr. Bodfish had himself suggested it in the professional hope that the person who had taken Mrs. Negget's gold brooch might try for further loot. He had, indeed, suggested baiting the dressing-table with the farmer's watch, an idea which Mr. Negget had promptly vetoed.

"I can't help thinking that Mrs. Pottle knows something about it," said Mrs. Negget, with an indignant glance at her husband.

"Mrs. Pottle," said the farmer, rising slowly and taking a seat on the oak settle built in the fireplace, "has been away from the village for near a fortnit."

"I didn't say she took it," snapped his wife. "I said I believe she knows something about it, and so I do. She's a horrid woman. Look at the way she encouraged her girl Looey to run after that young traveller from Smithson's. The whole fact of the matter is, it isn't your brooch, so you don't care."

"I said——" began Mr. Negget.

"I know what you said," retorted his wife, sharply, "and I wish you'd be quiet and not interrupt uncle. Here's my uncle been in the police twenty-five years, and you won't let him put a word in edgeways.'

"My way o' looking at it," said the ex-policeman, slowly, "is different to that o' the law; my idea is, an' always has been, that everybody is guilty until they've proved their innocence."

"It's a wonderful thing to me," said Mr. Negget in a low voice to his pipe, "as they should come to a house with a retired policeman living in it. Looks to me like somebody that ain't got much respect for the police."

The ex-policeman got up from the table, and taking a seat on the settle opposite the speaker, slowly filled a long clay and took a spill from the fireplace. His pipe lit, he turned to his niece, and slowly bade her go over the account of her loss once more.

"I missed it this morning," said Mrs. Negget, rapidly, "at ten minutes past twelve o'clock by the clock, and half-past five by my watch which wants looking to. I'd just put the batch of bread into the oven, and gone upstairs and opened the box that stands on my drawers to get a lozenge, and I missed the brooch."

"Do you keep it in that box?" asked the ex-policeman, slowly.

"Always," replied his niece. "I at once came down stairs and told Emma that the brooch had been stolen. I said that I named no names, and didn't wish to think bad of anybody, and that if I found the brooch back in the box when I went up stairs again, I should forgive whoever took it."

"And what did Emma say?" inquired Mr. Bodfish.

"Emma said a lot o' things," replied Mrs. Negget, angrily. "I'm sure by the lot she had to say you'd ha' thought she was the missis and me the servant. I gave her a month's notice at once, and she went straight up stairs and sat on her box and cried."

"Sat on her box?" repeated the ex-constable, impressively. "Oh!"

"That's what I thought," said his niece, "but it wasn't, because I got her off at last and searched it through and through. I never saw anything like her clothes in all my life. There was hardly a button or a tape on; and as for her stockings——"

"She don't get much time," said Mr. Negget, slowly.

"That's right; I thought you'd speak up for her," cried his wife, shrilly.

"Look here——" began Mr. Negget, laying his pipe on the seat by his side and rising slowly.

"Keep to the case in hand," said the ex-constable, waving him back to his seat again. "Now, Lizzie."

"I searched her box through and through," said his niece, "but it wasn't there; then I came down again and had a rare good cry all to myself."

"That's the best way for you to have it," remarked Mr. Negget, feelingly.

Mrs. Negget's uncle instinctively motioned his niece to silence, and holding his chin in his hand, scowled frightfully in the intensity of thought.

"See a cloo?" inquired Mr. Negget, affably.

"You ought to be ashamed of yourself, George," said his wife, angrily; "speaking to uncle when he's looking like that."

Mr. Bodfish said nothing; it is doubtful

whether he even heard these remarks; but he drew a huge notebook from his pocket, and after vainly trying to point his pencil by suction, took a knife from the table and hastily sharpened it.

"Was the brooch there last night?" he inquired.

"It were," said Mr. Negget, promptly. "Lizzie made me get up just as the owd clock were striking twelve to get her a lozenge."

"It seems pretty certain that the brooch went since then," mused Mr. Bodfish.

"It would seem like it to a plain man," said Mr. Negget, guardedly.

"I should like to see the box," said Mr. Bodfish.

Mrs. Negget went up and fetched it and stood eyeing him eagerly as he raised the lid and inspected the contents. It contained only a few lozenges and some bone studs. Mr. Negget helped himself to a lozenge, and going back to his seat, breathed peppermint.

"Properly speaking, that ought not to have been touched," said the ex-constable, regarding him with some severity.

"Eh!" said the startled farmer, putting his finger to his lips.

"Never mind," said the other, shaking his head. "It's too late now."

"He doesn't care a bit," said Mrs. Negget, somewhat sadly. "He used to keep buttons in that box with the lozenges until one night he gave me one by mistake. Yes, you may laugh —I'm glad you can laugh."

Mr. Negget, feeling that his mirth was certainly ill-timed, shook for some time in a noble effort to control himself, and despairing at length, went into the back place to recover. Sounds of blows indicative of Emma slapping him on the back did not add to Mrs. Negget's serenity.

"The point is," said the ex-constable, "could anybody have come into your room while you was asleep and taken it?"

"No," said Mrs. Negget, decisively. I'm a very poor sleeper, and I'd have woke at once, but if a flock of elephants was to come in the room they wouldn't wake George. He'd sleep through anything."

"Except her feeling under my piller for her

handkerchief," corroborated Mr. Negget, returning to the sitting-room.

Mr. Bodfish waved them to silence, and again gave way to deep thought. Three times he took up his pencil, and laying it down again, sat and drummed on the table with his fingers. Then he arose, and with bent head walked slowly round and round the room until he stumbled over a stool.

"Nobody came to the house this morning, I suppose?" he said at length, resuming his seat.

"Only Mrs. Driver," said his niece.

"What time did she come?" inquired Mr. Bodfish.

"Here! look here!" interposed Mr. Negget. "I've known Mrs. Driver thirty year a'most."

"What time did she come?" repeated the ex-constable, pitilessly.

His niece shook her head. "It might have been eleven, and again it might have been earlier," she replied. "I was out when she came."

"Out!" almost shouted the other.

Mrs. Negget nodded.

"She was sitting in here when I came back."

Her uncle looked up and glanced at the door

behind which a small staircase led to the room above.

"What was to prevent Mrs. Driver going up there while you were away?" he demanded.

"I shouldn't like to think that of Mrs. Driver," said his niece, shaking her head; "but then in these days one never knows what might happen. Never. I've given up thinking about it. However, when I came back, Mrs. Driver was here, sitting in that very chair you are sitting in now."

Mr. Bodfish pursed up his lips and made another note. Then he took a spill from the fireplace, and lighting a candle, went slowly and carefully up the stairs. He found nothing on them but two caked rims of mud, and being too busy to notice Mr. Negget's frantic signalling, called his niece's attention to them.

"What do you think of that?" he demanded, triumphantly.

"Somebody's been up there," said his niece. "It isn't Emma, because she hasn't been outside the house all day; and it can't be George, because he promised me faithful he'd never go up there in his dirty boots."

Mr. Negget coughed, and approaching the stairs, gazed with the eye of a stranger at the relics as Mr. Bodfish hotly rebuked a suggestion of his niece's to sweep them up.

"Seems to me," said the conscience-stricken Mr. Negget, feebly, "as they're rather large for a woman."

"Mud cakes," said Mr. Bodfish, with his most professional manner; "a small boot would pick up a lot this weather."

"So it would," said Mr. Negget, and with brazen effrontery not only met his wife's eye without quailing, but actually glanced down at her boots.

Mr. Bodfish came back to his chair and ruminated. Then he looked up and spoke.

"It was missed this morning at ten minutes past twelve," he said, slowly; "it was there last night. At eleven o'clock you came in and found Mrs. Driver sitting in that chair."

"No, the one you're in," interrupted his niece.

"It don't signify," said her uncle. "Nobody else has been near the place, and Emma's box has been searched.

"Thoroughly searched," testified Mrs. Negget.

"Now the point is, what did Mrs. Driver come for this morning?" resumed the ex-constable. Did she come——"

He broke off and eyed with dignified surprise a fine piece of wireless telegraphy between husband and wife. It appeared that Mr. Negget sent off a humorous message with his left eye, the right being for some reason closed, to which Mrs. Negget replied with a series of frowns and staccato shakes of the head, which her husband found easily translatable. Under the austere stare of Mr. Bodfish their faces at once regained their wonted calm, and the ex-constable in a somewhat offended manner resumed his inquiries.

"Mrs. Driver has been here a good bit lately," he remarked, slowly.

Mr. Negget's eyes watered, and his mouth worked piteously.

"If you can't behave yourself, George——" began his wife, fiercely.

"What is the matter?" demanded Mr. Bod-

fish.   "I'm not aware that I've said anything
to be laughed at."

"No more you have, uncle," retorted his
niece; "only George is such a stupid.   He's
got an idea in his silly head that Mrs.
Driver—— But it's all nonsense, of course."

"I've merely got a bit of an idea that it's a
wedding-ring, not a brooch, Mrs. Driver is
after," said the farmer to the perplexed constable.

Mr. Bodfish looked from one to the other.
"But you always keep yours on, Lizzie, don't
you?" he asked.

"Yes, of course," replied his niece, hurriedly; "but George has always got such strange
ideas.   Don't take no notice of him."

Her uncle sat back in his chair, his face still
wrinkled perplexedly; then the wrinkles van-
ished suddenly, chased away by a huge glow,
and he rose wrathfully and towered over the
match-making Mr. Negget.   "How dare
you?" he gasped.

Mr. Negget made no reply, but in a coward-
ly fashion jerked his thumb toward his wife.

"Oh! George!   How can you say so?" said the latter.

"I should never ha' thought of it by myself," said the farmer; "but I think they'd make a very nice couple, and I'm sure Mrs. Driver thinks so."

The ex-constable sat down in wrathful confusion, and taking up his notebook again, watched over the top of it the silent charges and countercharges of his niece and her husband.

"If I put my finger on the culprit," he asked at length, turning to his niece, "what do you wish done to her?"

Mrs. Negget regarded him with an expression which contained all the Christian virtues rolled into one.

"Nothing," she said, softly.   "I only want my brooch back."

The ex-constable shook his head at this leniency.

"Well, do as you please," he said, slowly. "In the first place, I want you to ask Mrs. Driver here to tea to-morrow—oh, I don't mind Negget's ridiculous ideas—pity he hasn't got something better to think of; if she's guilty, I'll soon find it out. I'll play with her like a cat with a mouse. I'll make her convict herself."

"Look here!" said Mr. Negget, with sudden vigour. "I won't have it. I won't have no woman asked here to tea to be got at like that. There's only my friends comes here to tea, and if any friend stole anything o' mine, I'd be one o' the first to hush it up."

"If they were all like you, George," said his wife, angrily, "where would the law be?"

"Or the police?" demanded Mr. Bodfish, staring at him.

"I won't have it!" repeated the farmer, loudly. "I'm the law here, and I'm the police here. That little tiny bit o' dirt was off my boots, I dare say. I don't care if it was."

"Very good," said Mr. Bodfish, turning to his indignant niece; "if he likes to look at it that way, there's nothing more to be said. I only wanted to get your brooch back for you, that's all; but if he's against it——"

"I'm against your asking Mrs. Driver here to my house to be got at," said the farmer.

"O' course if you can find out who took the brooch, and get it back again anyway, that's another matter."

Mr. Bodfish leaned over the table toward his niece.

"If I get an opportunity, I'll search her cottage," he said, in a low voice. "Strictly speaking, it ain't quite a legal thing to do, o' course, but many o' the finest pieces of detective work have been done by breaking the law. If she's a kleptomaniac, it's very likely lying about somewhere in the house."

He eyed Mr. Negget closely, as though half expecting another outburst, but none being forthcoming, sat back in his chair again and smoked in silence, while Mrs. Negget, with a carpet-brush which almost spoke, swept the pieces of dried mud from the stairs.

Mr. Negget was the last to go to bed that night, and finishing his pipe over the dying fire, sat for some time in deep thought. He had from the first raised objections to the presence of Mr. Bodfish at the farm, but family affection, coupled with an idea of testamentary benefits, had so wrought with his wife that he had allowed her to have her own way. Now he half fancied that he saw a chance of getting rid of him. If he could only enable the widow to catch him searching her house, it was highly probable that the ex-constable would find the village somewhat too hot to hold him. He gave his right leg a congratulatory slap as he thought of it, and knocking the ashes from his pipe, went slowly up to bed.

He was so amiable next morning that Mr. Bodfish, who was trying to explain to Mrs. Negget the difference between theft and kleptomania, spoke before him freely. The ex-constable defined kleptomania as a sort of amiable weakness found chiefly among the upper circles, and cited the case of a lady of title whose love of diamonds, combined with great hospitality, was a source of much embarrassment to her guests.

For the whole of that day Mr. Bodfish hung about in the neighbourhood of the widow's cottage, but in vain, and it would be hard to say whether he or Mr. Negget, who had been discreetly shadowing him, felt the disappointment most. On the day following, however, the ex-constable from a distant hedge saw a friend of the widow's enter the cottage, and a little later both ladies emerged and walked up the road.

He watched them turn the corner, and then, with a cautious glance round, which failed, however, to discover Mr. Negget, the ex-constable strolled casually in the direction of the cottage, and approaching it from the rear, turned the handle of the door and slipped in.

He searched the parlour hastily, and then, after a glance from the window, ventured up stairs. And he was in the thick of his self-imposed task when his graceless nephew by marriage, who had met Mrs. Driver and referred pathetically to a raging thirst which he had hoped to have quenched with some of her home-brewed, brought the ladies hastily back again.

"I'll go round the back way," said the wily Negget as they approached the cottage. "I just want to have a look at that pig of yours."

He reached the back door at the same time as Mr. Bodfish, and placing his legs apart, held it firmly against the frantic efforts of the ex-constable. The struggle ceased suddenly, and the door opened easily just as Mrs. Driver and her friend appeared in the front room, and the farmer, with a keen glance at the door of the larder which had just closed, took a chair while his hostess drew a glass of beer from the barrel in the kitchen.

Mr. Negget drank gratefully and praised the brew.   From beer the conversation turned naturally to the police, and from the police to the listening Mr. Bodfish, who was economizing space by sitting on the bread-pan, and trembling with agitation.

"He's a lonely man," said Negget, shaking his head and glancing from the corner of his eye at the door of the larder.   In his wildest dreams he had not imagined so choice a position, and he resolved to give full play to an idea which suddenly occurred to him.

"I dare say," said Mrs. Driver, carelessly, conscious that her friend was watching her.

"And the heart of a little child," said Negget; "you wouldn't believe how simple he is."

Mrs. Clowes said that it did him credit, but, speaking for herself, she hadn't noticed it.

"He was talking about you night before last," said Negget, turning to his hostess; "not that that's anything fresh. He always is talking about you nowadays."

The widow coughed confusedly and told him not to be foolish.

"Ask my wife," said the farmer, impressively; "they were talking about you for hours. He's a very shy man is my wife's uncle, but you should see his face change when your name's mentioned."

As a matter of fact, Mr. Bodfish's face was at that very moment taking on a deeper shade of crimson.

"Everything you do seems to interest him," continued the farmer, disregarding Mrs. Driver's manifest distress; "he was asking Lizzie about your calling on Monday; how long you stayed, and where you sat; and after she'd told him, I'm blest if he didn't go and sit in the same chair!"

This romantic setting to a perfectly casual action on the part of Mr. Bodfish affected the widow visibly, but its effect on the ex-constable nearly upset the bread-pan.

"But here," continued Mr. Negget, with another glance at the larder, "he might go on like that for years. He's a wunnerful shy man— big, and gentle, and shy. He wanted Lizzie to ask you to tea yesterday."

"Now, Mr. Negget," said the blushing widow. "Do be quiet."

"Fact," replied the farmer; "solemn fact, I assure you. And he asked her whether you were fond of jewellery."

"I met him twice in the road near here yesterday," said Mrs. Clowes, suddenly. "Perhaps he was waiting for you to come out."

"I dare say," replied the farmer. "I shouldn't wonder but what he's hanging about somewhere near now, unable to tear himself away."

Mr. Bodfish wrung his hands, and his thoughts reverted instinctively to instances in his memory in which charges of murder had been altered by the direction of a sensible judge to manslaughter. He held his breath for the next words.

Mr. Negget drank a little more ale and looked at Mrs. Driver.

MRS. DRIVER FELL BACK BEFORE THE
EMERGING FORM OF MR. BODFISH.

"I wonder whether you've got a morsel of bread and cheese?" he said, slowly. "I've come over that hungry——"

The widow and Mr. Bodfish rose simultaneously. It required not the brain of a trained detective to know that the cheese was in the larder. The unconscious Mrs. Driver opened the door, and then with a wild scream fell back before the emerging form of Mr. Bodfish into the arms of Mrs. Clowes. The glass of Mr. Negget smashed on the floor, and the farmer himself, with every appearance of astonishment, stared at the apparition open-mouthed.

"Mr.—Bodfish!" he said at length, slowly.

Mr. Bodfish, incapable of speech, glared at him ferociously.

"Leave him alone," said Mrs. Clowes, who was ministering to her friend. "Can't you see the man's upset at frightening her? She's coming round, Mr. Bodfish; don't be alarmed."

"Very good," said the farmer, who found his injured relative's gaze somewhat trying. "I'll go, and leave him to explain to Mrs. Driver why he was hidden in her larder. It don't seem a proper thing to me."

"Why, you silly man," said Mrs. Clowes, gleefully, as she paused at the door, "that don't want any explanation. Now, Mr. Bodfish, we're giving you your chance. Mind you make the most of it, and don't be too shy."

She walked excitedly up the road with the farmer, and bidding him good-bye at the corner, went off hastily to spread the news. Mr. Negget walked home soberly, and hardly staying long enough to listen to his wife's account of the finding of the brooch between the chest of drawers and the wall, went off to spend the evening with a friend, and ended by making a night of it.

In the Library

IN THE LIBRARY

THE fire had burnt low in the library, for the night was wet and warm. It was now little more than a grey shell, and looked desolate. Trayton Burleigh, still hot, rose from his armchair, and turning out one of the gas-jets, took a cigar from a box on a side-table and resumed his seat again.

The apartment, which was on the third floor at the back of the house, was a combination of library, study, and smoke-room, and was the daily despair of the old housekeeper who, with the assistance of one servant, managed the house. It was a bachelor establishment, and had been left to Trayton Burleigh and James Fletcher by a distant connection of both men some ten years before.

Trayton Burleigh sat back in his chair watching the smoke of his cigar through half-closed eyes.   Occasionally he opened them a little wider and glanced round the comfortable, well-furnished room, or stared with a cold gleam of hatred at Fletcher as he sat sucking stolidly at his brier pipe.   It was a comfortable room and a valuable house, half of which belonged to Trayton Burleigh; and yet he was to leave it in the morning and become a rogue and a wanderer over the face of the earth.   James Fletcher had said so.   James Fletcher, with the pipe still between his teeth and speaking from one corner of his mouth only, had pronounced his sentence.

"It hasn't occurred to you, I suppose," said Burleigh, speaking suddenly, "that I might refuse your terms."

"No," said Fletcher, simply.

Burleigh took a great mouthful of smoke and let it roll slowly out.

"I am to go out and leave you in possession?" he continued.   "You will stay here sole proprietor of the house; you will stay at the office sole owner and representative of the firm?   You are a good hand at a deal, James Fletcher."

"I am an honest man," said Fletcher, "and to raise sufficient money to make your defalcations good will not by any means leave me the gainer, as you very well know."

"There is no necessity to borrow," began Burleigh, eagerly. "We can pay the interest easily, and in course of time make the principal good without a soul being the wiser."

"That you suggested before," said Fletcher, "and my answer is the same. I will be no man's confederate in dishonesty; I will raise every penny at all costs, and save the name of the firm—and yours with it—but I will never have you darken the office again, or sit in this house after to-night."

"*You* won't," cried Burleigh, starting up in a frenzy of rage.

"*I* won't," said Fletcher. "You can choose the alternative: disgrace and penal servitude. Don't stand over me; you won't frighten me, I can assure you. Sit down."

"You have arranged so many things in your kindness," said Burleigh, slowly, resuming his seat again, "have you arranged how I am to live?"

"You have two strong hands, and health," replied Fletcher. "I will give you the two hundred pounds I mentioned, and after that you must look out for yourself. You can take it now."

He took a leather case from his breast pocket, and drew out a roll of notes. Burleigh, watching him calmly, stretched out his hand and took them from the table. Then he gave way to a sudden access of rage, and crumpling them in his hand, threw them into a corner of the room. Fletcher smoked on.

"Mrs. Marl is out?" said Burleigh, suddenly.

Fletcher nodded.

"She will be away the night," he said, slowly; "and Jane too; they have gone together somewhere, but they will be back at half-past eight in the morning."

"You are going to let me have one more breakfast in the old place, then," said Burleigh. "Half-past eight, half-past——"

He rose from his chair again. This time Fletcher took his pipe from his mouth and watched him closely. Burleigh stooped, and picking up the notes, placed them in his pocket.

"If I am to be turned adrift, it shall not be to leave you here," he said, in a thick voice.

He crossed over and shut the door; as he turned back Fletcher rose from his chair and stood confronting him. Burleigh put his hand to the wall, and drawing a small Japanese sword from its sheath of carved ivory, stepped slowly toward him.

"I give you one chance, Fletcher," he said, grimly. "You are a man of your word. Hush this up and let things be as they were before, and you are safe."

"Put that down," said Fletcher, sharply.

"By ——, I mean what I say!" cried the other.

"I mean what I said!" answered Fletcher.

He looked round at the last moment for a weapon, then he turned suddenly at a sharp sudden pain, and saw Burleigh's clenched fist nearly touching his breast-bone. The hand came away from his breast again, and something with it. It went a long way off. Trayton Burleigh suddenly went to a great distance and the room darkened. It got quite dark, and

Fletcher, with an attempt to raise his hands, let them fall to his side instead, and fell in a heap to the floor.

He was so still that Burleigh could hardly realize that it was all over, and stood stupidly waiting for him to rise again. Then he took out his handkerchief as though to wipe the sword, and thinking better of it, put it back into his pocket again, and threw the weapon on to the floor.

The body of Fletcher lay where it had fallen, the white face turned up to the gas. In life he had been a commonplace-looking man, not to say vulgar; now——

Burleigh, with a feeling of nausea, drew back toward the door, until the body was hidden by the table, and relieved from the sight, he could think more clearly. He looked down carefully and examined his clothes and his boots. Then he crossed the room again, and with his face averted, turned out the gas. Something seemed to stir in the darkness, and with a faint cry he blundered toward the door before he had realized that it was the clock. It struck twelve.

BURLEIGH, WITH A FEELING OF NAUSEA,
DREW BACK TOWARD THE DOOR.

He stood at the head of the stairs trying to recover himself; trying to think.   The gas on the landing below, the stairs and the furniture, all looked so prosaic and familiar that he could not realize what had occurred.   He walked slowly down and turned the light out.   The darkness of the upper part of the house was now almost appalling, and in a sudden panic he ran down stairs into the lighted hall, and snatching a hat from the stand, went to the door and walked down to the gate.

Except for one window the neighbouring houses were in darkness, and the lamps shone up a silent street.   There was a little rain in the air, and the muddy road was full of pebbles.   He stood at the gate trying to screw up his courage to enter the house again.   Then he noticed a figure coming slowly up the road and keeping close to the palings.

The full realization of what he had done broke in upon him when he found himself turning to fly from the approach of the constable. The wet cape glistening in the lamplight, the slow, heavy step, made him tremble.   Suppose the thing upstairs was not quite dead and should cry out? Suppose the constable should think it strange for him to be standing there and follow him in? He assumed a careless attitude, which did not feel careless, and as the man passed bade him good-night, and made a remark as to the weather.

Ere the sound of the other's footsteps had gone quite out of hearing, he turned and entered the house again before the sense of companionship should have quite departed. The first flight of stairs was lighted by the gas in the hall, and he went up slowly. Then he struck a match and went up steadily, past the library door, and with firm fingers turned on the gas in his bedroom and lit it. He opened the window a little way, and sitting down on his bed, tried to think.

He had got eight hours. Eight hours and two hundred pounds in small notes. He opened his safe and took out all the loose cash it contained, and walking about the room, gathered up and placed in his pockets such articles of jewellery as he possessed.

The first horror had now to some extent passed, and was succeeded by the fear of death.

With this fear on him he sat down again and tried to think out the first moves in that game of skill of which his life was the stake. He had often read of —— people of hasty temper, evading the police for a time, and eventually falling into their hands for lack of the most elementary common sense. He had heard it said that they always made some stupid blunder, left behind them some damning clue. He took his revolver from a drawer and saw that it was loaded. If the worst came to the worst, he would die quickly.

Eight hours' start; two hundred odd pounds. He would take lodgings at first in some populous district, and let the hair on his face grow. When the hue-and-cry had ceased, he would go abroad and start life again. He would go out of a night and post letters to himself, or better still, postcards, which his landlady would read. Postcards from cheery friends, from a sister, from a brother. During the day he would stay in and write, as became a man who described himself as a journalist.

Or suppose he went to the sea? Who would

look for him in flannels, bathing and boating with ordinary happy mortals? He sat and pondered. One might mean life, and the other death. Which?

His face burned as he thought of the responsibility of the choice. So many people went to the sea at that time of year that he would surely pass unnoticed. But at the sea one might meet acquaintances. He got up and nervously paced the room again. It was not so simple, now that it meant so much, as he had thought.

The sharp little clock on the mantel-piece rang out "one," followed immediately by the deeper note of that in the library. He thought of the clock, it seemed the only live thing in that room, and shuddered. He wondered whether the thing lying by the far side of the table heard it. He wondered——

He started and held his breath with fear. Somewhere down stairs a board creaked loudly, then another. He went to the door, and opening it a little way, but without looking out, listened. The house was so still that he could hear the ticking of the old clock in the kitchen below. He opened the door a little wider and peeped out. As he did so there was a sudden sharp outcry on the stairs, and he drew back into the room and stood trembling before he had quite realized that the noise had been made by the cat. The cry was unmistakable; but what had disturbed it?

There was silence again, and he drew near the door once more. He became certain that something was moving stealthily on the stairs. He heard the boards creak again, and once the rails of the balustrade rattled. The silence and suspense were frightful. Suppose that the something which had been Fletcher waited for him in the darkness outside?

He fought his fears down, and opening the door, determined to see what was beyond. The light from his room streamed out on to the landing, and he peered about fearfully. Was it fancy, or did the door of Fletcher's room opposite close as he looked? Was it fancy, or did the handle of the door really turn?

In perfect silence, and watching the door as he moved, to see that nothing came out and followed him, he proceeded slowly down the dark stairs. Then his jaw fell, and he turned

sick and faint again.   The library door, which
he distinctly remembered closing, and which,
moreover, he had seen was closed when he
went up stairs to his room, now stood open
some four or five inches.   He fancied that there
was a rustling inside, but his brain refused to
be certain.   Then plainly and unmistakably he
heard a chair pushed against the wall.

He crept to the door, hoping to pass it before
the thing inside became aware of his presence.
Something crept stealthily about the room.
With a sudden impulse he caught the handle of
the door, and, closing it violently, turned the
key in the lock, and ran madly down the stairs.

A fearful cry sounded from the room, and a
heavy hand beat upon the panels of the door.
The house rang with the blows, but above them
sounded the loud hoarse cries of human fear.
Burleigh, half-way down to the hall, stopped
with his hand on the balustrade and listened.
The beating ceased, and a man's voice cried out
loudly for God's sake to let him out.

At once Burleigh saw what had happened
and what it might mean for him.   He had left
the hall door open after his visit to the front,

and some wandering bird of the night had entered the house. No need for him to go now.
No need to hide either from the hangman's
rope or the felon's cell. The fool above had
saved him. He turned and ran up stairs again
just as the prisoner in his furious efforts to
escape wrenched the handle from the door.

"Who's there?" he cried, loudly.

"Let me out!" cried a frantic voice. "For
God's sake, open the door! There's something
here."

"Stay where you are!" shouted Burleigh,
sternly. "Stay where you are! If you come
out, I'll shoot you like a dog!"

The only response was a smashing blow on
the lock of the door. Burleigh raised his pistol, and aiming at the height of a man's chest,
fired through the panel.

The report and the crashing of the wood
made one noise, succeeded by an unearthly stillness, then the noise of a window hastily
opened. Burleigh fled hastily down the stairs,
and flinging wide the hall door, shouted loudly
for assistance.

It happened that a sergeant and the constable on the beat had just met in the road. They came toward the house at a run. Burleigh, with incoherent explanations, ran up stairs before them, and halted outside the library door. The prisoner was still inside, still trying to demolish the lock of the sturdy oaken door. Burleigh tried to turn the key, but the lock was too damaged to admit of its moving. The sergeant drew back, and, shoulder foremost, hurled himself at the door and burst it open.

He stumbled into the room, followed by the constable, and two shafts of light from the lanterns at their belts danced round the room. A man lurking behind the door made a dash for it, and the next instant the three men were locked together.

Burleigh, standing in the doorway, looked on coldly, reserving himself for the scene which was to follow. Except for the stumbling of the men and the sharp catch of the prisoner's breath, there was no noise. A helmet fell off and bounced and rolled along the floor. The men fell; there was a sobbing snarl and a sharp click. A tall figure rose from the floor; the other, on his knees, still held the man down. The standing figure felt in his pocket, and, striking a match, lit the gas.

The light fell on the flushed face and fair beard of the sergeant. He was bare-headed, and his hair dishevelled. Burleigh entered the room and gazed eagerly at the half-insensible man on the floor—a short, thick-set fellow with a white, dirty face and a black moustache. His lip was cut and bled down his neck. Burleigh glanced furtively at the table. The cloth had come off in the struggle, and was now in the place where he had left Fletcher.

"Hot work, sir," said the sergeant, with a smile. "It's fortunate we were handy."

The prisoner raised a heavy head and looked up with unmistakable terror in his eyes.

"All right, sir," he said, trembling, as the constable increased the pressure of his knee. "I 'ain't been in the house ten minutes altogether. By ——, I've not."

The sergeant regarded him curiously.

"It don't signify," he said, slowly; "ten minutes or ten seconds won't make any difference."

The man shook and began to whimper.

"It was 'ere when I come," he said, eagerly; "take that down, sir. I've only just come, and it was 'ere when I come. I tried to get away then, but I was locked in."

"What was?" demanded the sergeant.

"*That*," he said, desperately.

The sergeant, following the direction of the terror-stricken black eyes, stooped by the table. Then, with a sharp exclamation, he dragged away the cloth. Burleigh, with a sharp cry of horror, reeled back against the wall.

"All right, sir," said the sergeant, catching him; "all right. Turn your head away."

He pushed him into a chair, and crossing the room, poured out a glass of whiskey and brought it to him. The glass rattled against his teeth, but he drank it greedily, and then groaned faintly. The sergeant waited patiently. There was no hurry.

"Who is it, sir?" he asked at length.

"My friend—Fletcher," said Burleigh, with an effort. "We lived together." He turned to the prisoner.

"You damned villain!"

"He was dead when I come in the room, gentlemen," said the prisoner, strenuously. "He was on the floor dead, and when I see 'im, I tried to get out. S' 'elp me he was. You heard me call out, sir. I shouldn't ha' called out if I'd killed him."

"All right," said the sergeant, gruffly; "you'd better hold your tongue, you know."

"You keep quiet," urged the constable.

The sergeant knelt down and raised the dead man's head.

"I 'ad nothing to do with it," repeated the man on the floor. "I 'ad nothing to do with it. I never thought of such a thing. I've only been in the place ten minutes; put that down, sir."

The sergeant groped with his left hand, and picking up the Japanese sword, held it at him.

"I've never seen it before," said the prisoner, struggling.

"It used to hang on the wall," said Burleigh. "He must have snatched it down. It was on the wall when I left Fletcher a little while ago."

"How long?" inquired the sergeant.

"Perhaps an hour, perhaps half an hour," was the reply. "I went to my bedroom."

The man on the floor twisted his head and regarded him narrowly.

"You done it!" he cried, fiercely. "You done it, and you want me to swing for it."

"That 'll do," said the indignant constable.

The sergeant let his burden gently to the floor again.

"You hold your tongue, you devil!" he said, menacingly.

He crossed to the table and poured a little spirit into a glass and took it in his hand. Then he put it down again and crossed to Burleigh.

"Feeling better, sir?" he asked.

The other nodded faintly.

"You won't want this thing any more," said the sergeant.

He pointed to the pistol which the other still held, and taking it from him gently, put it into his pocket.

"You've hurt your wrist, sir," he said, anxiously.

Burleigh raised one hand sharply, and then the other.

"This one, I think," said the sergeant.   "I saw it just now."

He took the other's wrists in his hand, and suddenly holding them in the grip of a vice, whipped out something from his pocket— something hard and cold, which snapped suddenly on Burleigh's wrists, and held them fast.

"That's right," said the sergeant; "keep quiet."

The constable turned round in amaze; Burleigh sprang toward him furiously.

"Take these things off!" he choked.   "Have you gone mad?   Take them off!"

"All in good time," said the sergeant.

"Take them off!" cried Burleigh again.

For answer the sergeant took him in a powerful grip, and staring steadily at his white face and gleaming eyes, forced him to the other end of the room and pushed him into a chair.

"Collins," he said, sharply.

"Sir?" said the astonished subordinate.

"Run to the doctor at the corner hard as you can run!" said the other.   *This man is not dead!*

As the man left the room the sergeant took

up the glass of spirits he had poured out, and kneeling down by Fletcher again, raised his head and tried to pour a little down his throat. Burleigh, sitting in his corner, watched like one in a trance. He saw the constable return with the breathless surgeon, saw the three men bending over Fletcher, and then saw the eyes of the dying man open and the lips of the dying man move. He was conscious that the sergeant made some notes in a pocket-book, and that all three men eyed him closely. The sergeant stepped toward him and placed his hand on his shoulder, and obedient to the touch, he arose and went with him out into the night.

Captain Rogers

CAPTAIN ROGERS

A MAN came slowly over the old stone bridge, and averting his gaze from the dark river with its silent craft, looked with some satisfaction toward the feeble lights of the small town on the other side. He walked with the painful, forced step of one who has already trudged far. His worsted hose, where they were not darned, were in holes, and his coat and kneebreeches were rusty with much wear, but he straightened himself as he reached the end of the bridge and stepped out bravely to the taverns which stood in a row facing the quay.

He passed the "Queen Anne"—a mere beer-shop—without pausing, and after a glance apiece at the "Royal George" and the "Trusty Anchor," kept on his way to where the "Golden Key" hung out a gilded emblem. It was the best house in Riverstone, and patronized by the gentry, but he adjusted his faded coat, and with a swaggering air entered and walked boldly into the coffee-room.

The room was empty, but a bright fire afforded a pleasant change to the chill October air outside. He drew up a chair, and placing his feet on the fender, exposed his tattered soles to the blaze, as a waiter who had just seen him enter the room came and stood aggressively inside the door.

"Brandy and water," said the stranger; "hot."

"The coffee-room is for gentlemen staying in the house," said the waiter.

The stranger took his feet from the fender, and rising slowly, walked toward him. He was a short man and thin, but there was something so menacing in his attitude, and something so fearsome in his stony brown eyes, that the other, despite his disgust for ill-dressed people, moved back uneasily.

"Brandy and water, hot," repeated the stranger; "and plenty of it. D'ye hear?"

The man turned slowly to depart.

"Stop!" said the other, imperiously. "What's the name of the landlord here?"

"Mullet," said the fellow, sulkily.

"Send him to me," said the other, resuming his seat; "and hark you, my friend, more civility, or 'twill be the worse for you."

He stirred the log on the fire with his foot until a shower of sparks whirled up the chimney. The door opened, and the landlord, with the waiter behind him, entered the room, but he still gazed placidly at the glowing embers.

"What do you want?" demanded the landlord, in a deep voice.

The stranger turned a little weazened yellow face and grinned at him familiarly.

"Send that fat rascal of yours away," he said, slowly.

The landlord started at his voice and eyed him closely; then he signed to the man to withdraw, and closing the door behind him, stood silently watching his visitor.

"You didn't expect to see me, Rogers," said the latter.

"My name's Mullet," said the other, sternly. "What do you want?"

"Oh, Mullet?" said the other, in surprise. "I'm afraid I've made a mistake, then. I thought you were my old shipmate, Captain Rogers. It's a foolish mistake of mine, as I've no doubt Rogers was hanged years ago. You never had a brother named Rogers, did you?"

"I say again, what do you want?" demanded the other, advancing upon him.

"Since you're so good," said the other. "I want new clothes, food, and lodging of the best, and my pockets filled with money."

"You had better go and look for all those things, then," said Mullet. "You won't find them here."

"Ay!" said the other, rising. "Well, well! There was a hundred guineas on the head of my old shipmate Rogers some fifteen years ago. I'll see whether it has been earned yet."

"If I gave you a hundred guineas," said the innkeeper, repressing his passion by a mighty effort, "you would not be satisfied."

"Reads like a book," said the stranger, in tones of pretended delight. "What a man it is!"

He fell back as he spoke, and thrusting his

hand into his pocket, drew forth a long pistol as the innkeeper, a man of huge frame, edged toward him.

"Keep your distance," he said, in a sharp, quick voice.

The innkeeper, in no wise disturbed at the pistol, turned away calmly, and ringing the bell, ordered some spirits. Then taking a chair, he motioned to the other to do the same, and they sat in silence until the staring waiter had left the room again. The stranger raised his glass.

"My old friend Captain Rogers," he said, solemnly, "and may he never get his deserts!"

"From what jail have you come?" inquired Mullet, sternly.

"'Pon my soul," said the other, "I have been in so many—looking for Captain Rogers—that I almost forget the last, but I have just tramped from London, two hundred and eighty odd miles, for the pleasure of seeing your damned ugly figure-head again; and now I've found it, I'm going to stay. Give me some money."

The innkeeper, without a word, drew a little

gold and silver from his pocket, and placing it on the table, pushed it toward him.

"Enough to go on with," said the other, pocketing it; "in future it is halves. D'ye hear me? *Halves!* And I'll stay here and see I get it."

He sat back in his chair, and meeting the other's hatred with a gaze as steady as his own, replaced his pistol.

"A nice snug harbor after our many voyages," he continued. "Shipmates we were, shipmates we'll be; while Nick Gunn is alive you shall never want for company. Lord! Do you remember the Dutch brig, and the fat frightened mate?"

"I have forgotten it," said the other, still eyeing him steadfastly.   "I have forgotten many things.   For fifteen years I have lived a decent, honest life. Pray God for your own sinful soul, that the devil in me does not wake again."

"Fifteen years is a long nap," said Gunn, carelessly; "what a godsend it 'll be for you to have me by you to remind you of old times! Why, you're looking smug, man; the

GUNN PLACED A HAND, WHICH LACKED TWO
FINGERS, ON HIS BREAST AND BOWED AGAIN.

honest innkeeper to the life!   Gad! who's the girl?"

He rose and made a clumsy bow as a girl of eighteen, after a moment's hesitation at the door, crossed over to the innkeeper.

"I'm busy, my dear," said the latter, somewhat sternly.

"Our business," said Gunn, with another bow, "is finished. Is this your daughter, Rog— Mullet?"

"My stepdaughter," was the reply.

Gunn placed a hand, which lacked two fingers, on his breast, and bowed again.

"One of your father's oldest friends," he said smoothly; " and fallen on evil days; I'm sure your gentle heart will be pleased to hear that your good father has requested me—for a time—to make his house my home."

"Any friend of my father's is welcome to me, sir," said the girl, coldly. She looked from the innkeeper to his odd-looking guest, and conscious of something strained in the air, gave him a little bow and quitted the room.

"You insist upon staying, then?" said Mullet, after a pause.

"More than ever," replied Gunn, with a leer toward the door. "Why, you don't think I'm *afraid,* Captain? You should know me better than that."

"Life is sweet," said the other.

"Ay," assented Gunn, "so sweet that you will share things with me to keep it."

"No," said the other, with great calm. "I am man enough to have a better reason."

"No psalm singing," said Gunn, coarsely. "And look cheerful, you old buccaneer. Look as a man should look who has just met an old friend never to lose him again."

He eyed his man expectantly and put his hand to his pocket again, but the innkeeper's face was troubled, and he gazed stolidly at the fire.

"See what fifteen years' honest, decent life does for us," grinned the intruder.

The other made no reply, but rising slowly, walked to the door without a word.

"Landlord," cried Gunn, bringing his maimed hand sharply down on the table.

The innkeeper turned and regarded him.

"Send me in some supper," said Gunn; "the

best you have, and plenty of it, and have a room prepared.   The best."

The door closed silently, and was opened a little later by the dubious George coming in to set a bountiful repast.   Gunn, after cursing him for his slowness and awkwardness, drew his chair to the table and made the meal of one seldom able to satisfy his hunger.   He finished at last, and after sitting for some time smoking, with his legs sprawled on the fender, rang for a candle and demanded to be shown to his room.

His proceedings when he entered it were but a poor compliment to his host.   Not until he had poked and pried into every corner did he close the door.   Then, not content with locking it, he tilted a chair beneath the handle, and placing his pistol beneath his pillow, fell fast asleep.

Despite his fatigue he was early astir next morning.   Breakfast was laid for him in the coffee-room, and his brow darkened.   He walked into the hall, and after trying various doors entered a small sitting-room, where his host and daughter sat at breakfast, and with an easy assurance drew a chair to the table. The innkeeper helped him without a word, but the girl's hand shook under his gaze as she passed him some coffee.

"As soft a bed as ever I slept in," he remarked.

"I hope that you slept well," said the girl, civilly.

"Like a child," said Gunn, gravely; "an easy conscience. Eh, Mullet?"

The innkeeper nodded and went on eating. The other, after another remark or two, followed his example, glancing occasionally with warm approval at the beauty of the girl who sat at the head of the table.

"A sweet girl," he remarked, as she withdrew at the end of the meal; "and no mother, I presume?"

"No mother," repeated the other.

Gunn sighed and shook his head.

"A sad case, truly," he murmured. "No mother and such a guardian. Poor soul, if she but knew! Well, we must find her a husband."

He looked down as he spoke, and catching

sight of his rusty clothes and broken shoes, clapped his hand to his pocket; and with a glance at his host, sallied out to renew his wardrobe. The innkeeper, with an inscrutable face, watched him down the quay, then with bent head he returned to the house and fell to work on his accounts.

In this work Gunn, returning an hour later, clad from head to foot in new apparel, offered to assist him. Mullett hesitated, but made no demur; neither did he join in the ecstasies which his new partner displayed at the sight of the profits. Gunn put some more gold into his new pockets, and throwing himself back in a chair, called loudly to George to bring him some drink.

In less than a month the intruder was the virtual master of the "Golden Key." Resistance on the part of the legitimate owner became more and more feeble, the slightest objection on his part drawing from the truculent Gunn dark allusions to his past and threats against his future, which for the sake of his daughter he could not ignore. His health began to fail, and Joan watched with perplexed terror the growth of a situation which was in a fair way of becoming unbearable.

The arrogance of Gunn knew no bounds. The maids learned to tremble at his polite grin, or his worse freedom, and the men shrank appalled from his profane wrath. George, after ten years' service, was brutally dismissed, and refusing to accept dismissal from his hands, appealed to his master. The innkeeper confirmed it, and with lack-lustre eyes fenced feebly when his daughter, regardless of Gunn's presence, indignantly appealed to him.

"The man was rude to my friend, my dear," he said dispiritedly

"If he was rude, it was because Mr. Gunn deserved it," said Joan, hotly.

Gunn laughed uproariously.

"Gad, my dear, I like you!" he cried, slapping his leg. "You're a girl of spirit. Now I will make you a fair offer. If you ask for George to stay, stay he shall, as a favour to your sweet self."

The girl trembled.

"Who is master here?" she demanded, turning a full eye on her father.

Mullet laughed uneasily.

"This is business," he said, trying to speak lightly, "and women can't understand it. Gunn is—is valuable to me, and George must go."

"Unless you plead for him, sweet one?" said Gunn.

The girl looked at her father again, but he turned his head away and tapped on the floor with his foot. Then in perplexity, akin to tears, she walked from the room, carefully drawing her dress aside as Gunn held the door for her.

"A fine girl," said Gunn, his thin lips working; "a fine spirit. 'Twill be pleasant to break it; but she does not know who is master here."

"She is young yet," said the other, hurriedly.

"I will soon age her if she looks like that at me again," said Gunn. "By ——, I'll turn out the whole crew into the street, and her with them, an' I wish it. I'll lie in my bed warm o' nights and think of her huddled on a doorstep."

His voice rose and his fists clenched, but he kept his distance and watched the other warily. The innkeeper's face was contorted and his brow grew wet. For one moment something peeped out of his eyes; the next he sat down in his chair again and nervously fingered his chin.

"I have but to speak," said Gunn, regarding him with much satisfaction, "and you will hang, and your money go to the Crown. What will become of her then, think you?"

The other laughed nervously.

" 'Twould be stopping the golden eggs," he ventured.

"Don't think too much of that," said Gunn, in a hard voice.   "I was never one to be baulked, as you know."

"Come, come. Let us be friends," said Mullet; "the girl is young, and has had her way."

He looked almost pleadingly at the other, and his voice trembled. Gunn drew himself up, and regarding him with a satisfied sneer, quitted the room without a word.

Affairs at the "Golden Key" grew steadily worse and worse. Gunn dominated the place, and his vile personality hung over it like a shadow. Appeals to the innkeeper were in vain; his health was breaking fast, and he moodily declined to interfere. Gunn appointed servants of his own choosing—brazen maids and foul-mouthed men. The old patrons ceased to frequent the "Golden Key," and its bedrooms stood empty. The maids scarcely deigned to take an order from Joan, and the men spoke to her familiarly. In the midst of all this the innkeeper, who had complained once or twice of vertigo, was seized with a fit.

Joan, flying to him for protection against the brutal advances of Gunn, found him lying in a heap behind the door of his small office, and in her fear called loudly for assistance. A little knot of servants collected, and stood regarding him stupidly. One made a brutal jest. Gunn, pressing through the throng, turned the senseless body over with his foot, and cursing vilely, ordered them to carry it upstairs.

Until the surgeon came, Joan, kneeling by the bed, held on to the senseless hand as her only protection against the evil faces of Gunn and his protégés. Gunn himself was taken aback, the innkeeper's death at that time by no means suiting his aims.

The surgeon was a man of few words and

fewer attainments, but under his ministrations the innkeeper, after a long interval, rallied. The half-closed eyes opened, and he looked in a dazed fashion at his surroundings. Gunn drove the servants away and questioned the man of medicine. The answers were vague and interspersed with Latin. Freedom from noise and troubles of all kinds was insisted upon and Joan was installed as nurse, with a promise of speedy assistance.

The assistance arrived late in the day in the shape of an elderly woman, wnose Spartan treatment of her patients had helped many along the silent road. She commenced her reign by punching the sick man's pillows, and having shaken him into consciousness by this means, gave him a dose of physic, after first tasting it herself from the bottle.

After the first rally the innkeeper began to fail slowly. It was seldom that he understood what was said to him, and pitiful to the beholder to see in his intervals of consciousness his timid anxiety to earn the good-will of the all-powerful Gunn. His strength declined until assistance was needed to turn him in the bed, and his great sinewy hands were forever trembling and fidgeting on the coverlet.

Joan, pale with grief and fear, tended him assiduously. Her stepfather's strength had been a proverb in the town, and many a hasty citizen had felt the strength of his arm. The increasing lawlessness of the house filled her with dismay, and the coarse attentions of Gunn became more persistent than ever. She took her meals in the sick-room, and divided her time between that and her own.

Gunn himself was in a dilemma. With Mullet dead, his power was at an end and his visions of wealth dissipated. He resolved to feather his nest immediately, and interviewed the surgeon. The surgeon was ominously reticent, the nurse cheerfully ghoulish.

"Four days I give him," she said, calmly; "four blessed days, not but what he might slip away at any moment."

Gunn let one day of the four pass, and then, choosing a time when Joan was from the room, entered it for a little quiet conversation. The innkeeper's eyes were open, and, what was more to the purpose, intelligent.

"You're cheating the hangman, after all," snarled Gunn. "I'm off to swear an information."

The other, by a great effort, turned his heavy head and fixed his wistful eyes on him.

"Mercy!" he whispered. "For her sake—give me—a little time!"

"To slip your cable, I suppose," quoth Gunn. "Where's your money? Where's your hoard, you miser?"

Mullet closed his eyes. He opened them again slowly and strove to think, while Gunn watched him narrowly. When he spoke, his utterance was thick and labored.

"Come to-night," he muttered, slowly. "Give me—time—I will make your—your fortune. But the nurse—watches."

"I'll see to her," said Gunn, with a grin. "But tell me now, lest you die first."

"You will—let Joan—have a share?" panted the innkeeper.

"Yes, yes," said Gunn, hastily.

The innkeeper strove to raise himself in the bed, and then fell back again exhausted as Joan's step was heard on the stairs. Gunn gave a savage glance of warning at him, and barring the progress of the girl at the door, attempted to salute her. Joan came in pale and trembling, and falling on her knees by the bedside, took her father's hand in hers and wept over it. The innkeeper gave a faint groan and a shiver ran through his body.

It was nearly an hour after midnight that Nick Gunn, kicking off his shoes, went stealthily out onto the landing. A little light came from the partly open door of the sick-room, but all else was in blackness. He moved along and peered in.

The nurse was siting in a high-backed oak chair by the fire. She had slipped down in the seat, and her untidy head hung on her bosom. A glass stood on the small oak table by her side, and a solitary candle on the high mantel-piece diffused a sickly light. Gunn entered the room, and finding that the sick man was dozing, shook him roughly.

The innkeeper opened his eyes and gazed at him blankly.

"Wake, you fool," said Gunn, shaking him again.

The other roused and muttered something incoherently.   Then he stirred slightly.

"The nurse," he whispered.

"She's safe enow," said Gunn.   "I've seen to that."

He crossed the room lightly, and standing before the unconscious woman, inspected her closely and raised her in the chair.   Her head fell limply over the arm.

"Dead?" inquired Mullet, in a fearful whisper.

"Drugged," said Gunn, shortly.   "Now speak up, and be lively."

The innkeeper's eyes again travelled in the direction of the nurse.

"The men," he whispered; "the servants."

"Dead drunk and asleep," said Gunn, biting the words.   "The last day would hardly rouse them.   Now will you speak, damn you!"

"I must—take care—of Joan," said the father.

Gunn shook his clenched hand at him.

"My money—is—is—" said the other. "Promise me on—your oath—Joan."

"Ay, ay," growled Gunn; "how many more

times? I'll marry her, and she shall have what I choose to give her. Speak up, you fool! It's not for you to make terms. Where is it?"

He bent over, but Mullet, exhausted with his efforts, had closed his eyes again, and half turned his head.

"Where is it, damn you?" said Gunn, from between his teeth.

Mullet opened his eyes again, glanced fearfully round the room, and whispered. Gunn, with a stifled oath, bent his ear almost to his mouth, and the next moment his neck was in the grip of the strongest man in Riverstone, and an arm like a bar of iron over his back pinned him down across the bed.

"You *dog!*" hissed a fierce voice in his ear. "I've got you—Captain Rogers at your service, and now you may tell his name to all you can. Shout it, you spawn of hell. Shout it!"

He rose in bed, and with a sudden movement flung the other over on his back. Gunn's eyes were starting from his head, and he writhed convulsively.

"I thought you were a sharper man, Gunn," said Rogers, still in the same hot whisper, as he relaxed his grip a little; "you are too simple, you hound! When you first threatened me I resolved to kill you. Then you threatened my daughter. I wish that you had nine lives, that I might take them all. Keep still!"

He gave a half-glance over his shoulder at the silent figure of the nurse, and put his weight on the twisting figure on the bed.

"You drugged the hag, good Gunn," he continued. "To-morrow morning, Gunn, they will find you in your room dead, and if one of the scum you brought into my house be charged with the murder, so much the better. When I am well they will go. I am already feeling a little bit stronger, Gunn, as you see, and in a month I hope to be about again."

He averted his face, and for a time gazed sternly and watchfully at the door. Then he rose slowly to his feet, and taking the dead man in his arms, bore him slowly and carefully to his room, and laid him a huddled heap on the floor. Swiftly and noiselessly he put the dead man's shoes on and turned his pockets inside out, kicked a rug out of place, and put a guinea on the floor. Then he stole cautiously down stairs and set a small door at the back open. A dog barked frantically, and he hurried back to his room. The nurse still slumbered by the fire.

She awoke in the morning shivering with the cold, and being jealous of her reputation, rekindled the fire, and measuring out the dose which the invalid should have taken, threw it away. On these unconscious preparations for an alibi Captain Rogers gazed through half-closed lids, and then turning his grim face to the wall, waited for the inevitable alarm.

A Tiger's Skin

A TIGER'S SKIN

THE travelling sign-painter who was re-painting the sign of the "Cauliflower" was enjoying a well-earned respite from his labours. On the old table under the shade of the elms mammoth sandwiches and a large slice of cheese waited in an untied handkerchief until such time as his thirst should be satisfied. At the other side of the table the oldest man in Claybury, drawing gently at a long clay pipe, turned a dim and regretful eye up at the old signboard.

"I've drunk my beer under it for pretty near seventy years," he said, with a sigh. "It's a pity it couldn't ha' lasted my time."

The painter, slowly pushing a wedge of sandwich into his mouth, regarded him indulgently.

"It's all through two young gentlemen as was passing through 'ere a month or two ago," continued the old man; "they told Smith, the landlord, they'd been looking all over the place for the 'Cauliflower,' and when Smith showed 'em the sign they said they thought it was the 'George the Fourth,' and a very good likeness, too."

The painter laughed and took another look at the old sign; then, with the nervousness of the true artist, he took a look at his own.   One or two shadows——

He flung his legs over the bench and took up his brushes.   In ten minutes the most fervent loyalist would have looked in vain for any resemblance, and with a sigh at the pitfalls which beset the artist he returned to his interrupted meal and hailed the house for more beer.

"There's nobody could mistake your sign for anything but a cauliflower," said the old man; "it looks good enough to eat."

The painter smiled and pushed his mug across the table.   He was a tender-hearted man, and once—when painting the sign of the "Sir Wilfrid Lawson"—knew himself what it was to lack beer.   He began to discourse on art, and spoke somewhat disparagingly of the cauliflower as a subject. With a shake of his head he spoke of the possibilities of a spotted cow or a blue lion.

"Talking of lions," said the ancient, musingly, "I s'pose as you never 'eard tell of the Claybury tiger? It was afore your time in these parts, I expect."

The painter admitted his ignorance, and, finding that the allusion had no reference to an inn, pulled out his pipe and prepared to listen.

"It's a while ago now," said the old man, slowly, "and the circus the tiger belonged to was going through Claybury to get to Wickham, when, just as they was passing Gill's farm, a steam-ingine they 'ad to draw some o' the vans broke down, and they 'ad to stop while the blacksmith mended it. That being so, they put up a big tent and 'ad the circus 'ere.

"I was one o' them as went, and I must say it was worth the money, though Henry Walker was disappointed at the man who put 'is 'ead in the lion's mouth. He said that the man frightened the lion first, before 'e did it.

"It was a great night for Claybury, and for

about a week nothing else was talked of. All the children was playing at being lions and tigers and such-like, and young Roberts pretty near broke 'is back trying to see if he could ride horseback standing up.

"It was about two weeks after the circus 'ad gone when a strange thing 'appened: the big tiger broke loose. Bill Chambers brought the news first, 'aving read it in the newspaper while 'e was 'aving his tea. He brought out the paper and showed us, and soon after we 'eard all sorts o' tales of its doings.

"At first we thought the tiger was a long way off, and we was rather amused at it. Frederick Scott laughed 'imself silly a'most up 'ere one night thinking 'ow surprised a man would be if 'e come 'ome one night and found the tiger sitting in his armchair eating the baby. It didn't seem much of a laughing matter to me, and I said so; none of us liked it, and even Sam Jones, as 'ad got twins for the second time, said 'Shame!' But Frederick Scott was a man as would laugh at anything.

"When we 'eard that the tiger 'ad been seen within three miles of Claybury things began to look serious, and Peter Gubbins said that something ought to be done, but before we could think of anything to do something 'appened.

"We was sitting up 'ere one evening 'aving a mug o' beer and a pipe—same as I might be now if I'd got any baccy left—and talking about it, when we 'eard a shout and saw a ragged-looking tramp running toward us as 'ard as he could run. Every now and then he'd look over 'is shoulder and give a shout, and then run 'arder than afore.

" 'It's the *tiger!*' ses Bill Chambers, and afore you could wink a'most he was inside the house, 'aving first upset Smith and a pot o' beer in the doorway.

"Before he could get up, Smith 'ad to wait till we was all in. His langwidge was awful for a man as 'ad a license to lose, and everybody shouting 'Tiger!' as they trod on 'im didn't ease 'is mind. He was inside a'most as soon as the last man, though, and in a flash he 'ad the door bolted just as the tramp flung 'imself agin it, all out of breath and sobbing 'is hardest to be let in.

" 'Open the door,' he ses, banging on it.

" 'Go away,' ses Smith.

" 'It's the tiger,' screams the tramp; 'open the door.'

" 'You go away,' ses Smith, 'you're attracting it to my place; run up the road and draw it off.' "

"Just at that moment John Biggs, the blacksmith, come in from the taproom, and as soon as he 'eard wot was the matter 'e took down Smith's gun from behind the bar and said he was going out to look after the wimmen and children.

" 'Open the door,' he ses.

"He was trying to get out and the tramp outside was trying to get in, but Smith held on to that door like a Briton.   Then John Biggs lost 'is temper, and he ups with the gun— Smith's own gun, mind you—and fetches 'im a bang over the 'ead with it.   Smith fell down at once, and afore we could 'elp ourselves the door was open, the tramp was inside, and John Biggs was running up the road, shouting 'is hardest.

"We 'ad the door closed afore you could wink a'most, and then, while the tramp lay in a corner 'aving brandy, Mrs. Smith got a bowl of water and a sponge and knelt down bathing 'er husband's 'ead with it.

" 'Did you see the tiger?' ses Bill Chambers.

" 'See it?' ses the tramp, with a shiver. 'Oh, Lord!'

"He made signs for more brandy, and Henery Walker, wot was acting as landlord, without being asked, gave it to 'im.

" 'It chased me for over a mile,' ses the tramp; 'my 'eart's breaking.'

"He gave a groan and fainted right off. A terrible faint it was, too, and for some time we thought 'ed never come round agin. First they poured brandy down 'is throat, then gin, and then beer, and still 'e didn't come round, but lay quiet with 'is eyes closed and a horrible smile on 'is face.

"He come round at last, and with nothing stronger than water, which Mrs. Smith kept pouring into 'is mouth. First thing we noticed was that the smile went, then 'is eyes opened, and suddenly 'e sat up with a shiver and gave such a dreadful scream that we thought at first the tiger was on top of us.

"Then 'e told us 'ow he was sitting washing 'is shirt in a ditch, when he 'eard a snuffling noise and saw the 'ead of a big tiger sticking through the hedge the other side.   He left 'is shirt and ran, and 'e said that, fortunately, the tiger stopped to tear the shirt to pieces, else 'is last hour would 'ave arrived.

"When 'e 'ad finished Smith went upstairs and looked out of the bedroom winders, but 'e couldn't see any signs of the tiger, and 'e said no doubt it 'ad gone down to the village to see wot it could pick up, or p'raps it 'ad eaten John Biggs.

"However that might be, nobody cared to go outside to see, and after it got dark we liked going 'ome less than ever.

"Up to ten o'clock we did very well, and then Smith began to talk about 'is license.   He said it was all rubbish being afraid to go 'ome, and that, at any rate, the tiger couldn't eat more than one of us, and while 'e was doing that there was the chance for the others to get 'ome safe.   Two or three of 'em took a dislike to Smith that night and told 'im so.

"The end of it was we all slept in the taproom that night.   It seemed strange at first, but anything was better than going 'ome in the dark, and we all slept till about four next morning, when we woke up and found the tramp 'ad gone and left the front door standing wide open.

"We took a careful look-out, and by-and-by first one started off and then another to see whether their wives and children 'ad been eaten or not.   Not a soul 'ad been touched, but the wimmen and children was that scared there was no doing anything with 'em.   None o' the children would go to school, and they sat at 'ome all day with the front winder blocked up with a mattress to keep the tiger out.

"Nobody liked going to work, but it 'ad to be done and as Farmer Gill said that tigers went to sleep all day and only came out toward evening we was a bit comforted.   Not a soul went up to the 'Cauliflower' that evening for fear of coming 'ome in the dark, but as nothing 'appened that night we began to 'ope as the tiger 'ad travelled further on.

"Bob Pretty laughed at the whole thing and said 'e didn't believe there was a tiger; but nobody minded wot 'e said, Bob Pretty being, as I've often told people, the black sheep o' Claybury, wot with poaching and, wot was worse, 'is artfulness.

"But the very next morning something 'appened that made Bob Pretty look silly and wish 'e 'adn't talked quite so fast; for at five o'clock Frederick Scott, going down to feed 'is hins, found as the tiger 'ad been there afore 'im and 'ad eaten no less than seven of 'em. The side of the hin-'ouse was all broke in, there was a few feathers lying on the ground, and two little chicks smashed and dead beside 'em.

"The way Frederick Scott went on about it you'd 'ardly believe. He said that Govinment 'ud 'ave to make it up to 'im, and instead o' going to work 'e put the two little chicks and the feathers into a pudding basin and walked to Cudford, four miles off, where they 'ad a policeman.

"He saw the policeman, William White by name, standing at the back door of the 'Fox and Hounds' public house, throwing a 'andful o' corn to the landlord's fowls, and the first thing Mr. White ses was, 'it's off my beat,' he ses.

" 'But you might do it in your spare time, Mr. White,' ses Frederick Scott. It's very likely that the tiger'll come back to my hin-'ouse for the rest of 'em, and he'd be very surprised if 'e popped 'is 'ead in and see you there waiting for 'im.'

"He'd 'ave reason to be,' ses Policeman White, staring at 'im.

" 'Think of the praise you'd get,' said Frederick Scott, coaxing like.

" 'Look 'ere,' ses Policeman White, 'if you don't take yourself and that pudding basin off pretty quick, you'll come along o' me, d'ye see? You've been drinking and you're in a excited state.'

"He gave Frederick Scott a push and follered 'im along the road, and every time Frederick stopped to ask 'im wot 'e was doing of 'e gave 'im another push to show 'im.

"Frederick Scott told us all about it that evening, and some of the bravest of us went up to the 'Cauliflower' to talk over wot was to be done, though we took care to get 'ome while it was quite light. That night Peter Gubbins's two pigs went. They were two o' the likeliest pigs I ever seed, and all Peter Gubbins could do was to sit up in bed shivering and listening to their squeals as the tiger dragged 'em off. Pretty near all Claybury was round that sty next morning looking at the broken fence. Some of them looked for the tiger's footmarks, but it was dry weather and they couldn't see any. Nobody knew whose turn it would be next, and the most sensible man there, Sam Jones, went straight off 'ome and killed his pig afore 'e went to work.

"Nobody knew what to do; Farmer Hall said as it was a soldier's job, and 'e drove over to Wickham to tell the police so, but nothing came of it, and that night at ten minutes to twelve Bill Chambers's pig went. It was one o' the biggest pigs ever raised in Claybury, but the tiger got it off as easy as possible. Bill 'ad the bravery to look out of the winder when 'e 'eard the pig squeal, but there was such a awful snarling noise that 'e daresn't move 'and or foot.

"Dicky Weed's idea was for people with pigs and such-like to keep 'em in the house of a night, but Peter Gubbins and Bill Chambers both pointed out that the tiger could break a back door with one blow of 'is paw, and that if 'e got inside he might take something else instead o' pig.   And they said that it was no worse for other people to lose pigs than wot it was for them.

"The odd thing about it was that all this time nobody 'ad ever seen the tiger except the tramp and people sent their children back to school agin and felt safe going about in the daytime till little Charlie Gubbins came running 'ome crying and saying that 'e'd seen it.   Next morning a lot more children see it and was afraid to go to school, and people began to wonder wot 'ud happen when all the pigs and poultry was eaten.

"Then Henery Walker see it.   We was sitting inside 'ere with scythes, and pitchforks, and such-like things handy, when we see 'im come in without 'is hat.   His eyes were staring and 'is hair was all rumpled.   He called for a pot o' ale and drank it nearly off, and then 'e sat gasping and 'olding the mug between 'is legs and shaking 'is 'ead at the floor till everybody 'ad left off talking to look at 'im.

" 'Wot's the matter, Henery?' ses one of 'em.

" 'Don't ask me,' ses Henery Walker, with a shiver.

" 'You don't mean to say as 'ow you've seen the tiger?'' ses Bill Chambers.

"Henery Walker didn't answer 'im. He got up and walked back'ards and for'ards, still with that frightened look in 'is eyes, and once or twice 'e give such a terrible start that 'e frightened us 'arf out of our wits. Then Bill Chambers took and forced 'im into a chair and give 'im two o' gin and patted 'im on the back, and at last Henery Walker got 'is senses back agin and told us 'ow the tiger 'ad chased 'im all round and round the trees in Plashett's Wood until 'e managed to climb up a tree and escape it. He said the tiger 'ad kept 'im there for over an hour, and then suddenly turned round and bolted off up the road to Wickham.

"It was a merciful escape, and everybody said so except Sam Jones, and 'e asked so many questions that at last Henery Walker asked 'im outright if 'e disbelieved 'is word.

" 'It's all right, Sam,' ses Bob Pretty, as 'ad

come in just after Henery Walker. 'I see 'im with the tiger after 'im.'

" 'Wot?' ses Henery, staring at him.

" 'I see it all, Henery,' ses Bob Pretty, 'and I see your pluck. It was all you could do to make up your mind to run from it. I believe if you'd 'ad a fork in your 'and you'd 'ave made a fight for it."

"Everybody said 'Bravo!'; but Henery Walker didn't seem to like it at all. He sat still, looking at Bob Pretty, and at last 'e ses, 'Where was you?' 'e ses.

" 'Up another tree, Henery, where you couldn't see me,' ses Bob Pretty, smiling at 'im.

Henery Walker, wot was drinking some beer, choked a bit, and then 'e put the mug down and went straight off 'ome without saying a word to anybody. I knew 'e didn't like Bob Pretty, but I couldn't see why 'e should be cross about 'is speaking up for 'im as 'e had done, but Bob said as it was 'is modesty, and 'e thought more of 'im for it.

After that things got worse than ever; the wimmen and children stayed indoors and kept the doors shut, and the men never knew when they went out to work whether they'd come 'ome agin. They used to kiss their children afore they went out of a morning, and their wives too, some of 'em; even men who'd been married for years did. And several more of 'em see the tiger while they was at work, and came running 'ome to tell about it.

"The tiger 'ad been making free with Claybury pigs and such-like for pretty near a week, and nothing 'ad been done to try and catch it, and wot made Claybury men madder than anything else was folks at Wickham saying it was all a mistake, and the tiger 'adn't escaped at all. Even parson, who'd been away for a holiday, said so, and Henery Walker told 'is wife that if she ever set foot inside the church agin 'ed ask 'is old mother to come and live with 'em.

"It was all very well for parson to talk, but the very night he come back Henery Walker's pig went, and at the same time George Kettle lost five or six ducks.

"He was a quiet man, was George, but when 'is temper was up 'e didn't care for anything. Afore he came to Claybury 'e 'ad been in the Militia, and that evening at the 'Cauliflower' 'e turned up with a gun over 'is shoulder and made a speech, and asked who was game to go with 'im and hunt the tiger. Bill Chambers, who was still grieving after 'is pig, said 'e would, then another man offered, until at last there was seventeen of 'em. Some of 'em 'ad scythes and some pitchforks, and one or two of 'em guns, and it was one o' the finest sights I ever seed when George Kettle stood 'em in rows of four and marched 'em off.

"They went straight up the road, then across Farmer Gill's fields to get to Plashett's wood, where they thought the tiger 'ud most likely be, and the nearer they got to the wood the slower they walked. The sun 'ad just gone down and the wood looked very quiet and dark, but John Biggs, the blacksmith, and George Kettle walked in first and the others follered, keeping so close together that Sam Jones 'ad a few words over his shoulder with Bill Chambers about the way 'e was carrying 'is pitchfork.

"Every now and then somebody 'ud say, '*Wot's that!*' and they'd all stop and crowd together and think the time 'ad come, but it 'adn't, and then they'd go on agin, trembling, until they'd walked all round the wood without seeing anything but one or two rabbits. John Biggs and George Kettle wanted for to stay there till it was dark, but the others wouldn't 'ear of it for fear of frightening their wives, and just as it was getting dark they all come tramp, tramp, back to the 'Cauliflower' agin.

"Smith stood 'em 'arf a pint apiece, and they was all outside 'ere fancying theirselves a bit for wot they'd done when we see old man Parsley coming along on two sticks as fast as 'e could come.

"'Are you brave lads a-looking for the tiger?' he asks.

"'Yes,' ses John Biggs.

"'Then 'urry up, for the sake of mercy,' ses old Mr. Parsley, putting 'is 'and on the table and going off into a fit of coughing; 'it's just gone into Bob Pretty's cottage. I was passing and saw it.'

"George Kettle snatches up 'is gun and shouts out to 'is men to come along. Some of 'em was for 'anging back at first, some because they didn't like the tiger and some because they didn't like Bob Pretty, but John Biggs drove 'em in front of 'im like a flock o' sheep and then they gave a cheer and ran after George Kettle, full pelt up the road.

"A few wimmen and children was at their doors as they passed, but they took fright and went indoors screaming. There was a lamp in Bob Pretty's front room, but the door was closed and the 'ouse was silent as the grave.

"George Kettle and the men with the guns went first, then came the pitchforks, and last of all the scythes. Just as George Kettle put 'is 'and on the door he 'eard something moving inside, and the next moment the door opened and there stood Bob Pretty.

" 'What the dickens!' 'e ses, starting back as 'e see the guns and pitchforks pointing at 'im.

" ''Ave you killed it, Bob?' ses George Kettle.

" 'Killed *wot?*' ses Bob Pretty. 'Be careful o' them guns. Take your fingers off the triggers.'

" 'The tiger's in your 'ouse, Bob,' ses George Kettle, in a whisper. ''Ave you on'y just come in?'

" 'Look 'ere,' ses Bob Pretty. 'I don't want

any o' your games. You go and play 'em somewhere else."

" 'It ain't a game,' ses John Biggs; 'the tiger's in your 'ouse and we're going to kill it. Now, then, lads.'

"They all went in in a 'eap, pushing Bob Pretty in front of 'em, till the room was full. Only one man with a scythe got in, and they wouldn't 'ave let 'im in if they'd known. It a'most made 'em forget the tiger for the time.

"George Kettle opened the door wot led into the kitchen, and then 'e sprang back with such a shout that the man with the scythe tried to escape, taking Henery Walker along with 'im. George Kettle tried to speak, but couldn't. All 'e could do was to point with 'is finger at Bob Pretty's kitchen—*and Bob Pretty's kitchen was for all the world like a pork-butcher's shop*. There was joints o' pork 'anging from the ceiling, two brine tubs as full as they could be, and quite a string of fowls and ducks all ready for market.

" 'Wot d'ye mean by coming into my 'ouse?' ses Bob Pretty, blustering. 'If you don't clear out pretty quick, I'll make you.'

"Nobody answered 'im; they was all examining 'ands o' pork and fowls and such-like.

" 'There's the tiger,' ses Henery Walker, pointing at Bob Pretty; 'that's wot old man Parsley meant.'

" 'Somebody go and fetch Policeman White,' ses a voice.

" 'I wish they would,' ses Bob Pretty. "I'll 'ave the law on you all for breaking into my 'ouse like this, see if I don't.'

" 'Where'd you get all this pork from?' ses the blacksmith.

" 'And them ducks and hins?' ses George Kettle.

" 'That's my bisness,' ses Bob Pretty, staring 'em full in the face. 'I just 'ad a excellent oppertunity offered me of going into the pork and poultry line and I took it. Now, all them as doesn't want to buy any pork or fowls go out o' my house.'

" 'You're a thief, Bob Pretty!' says Henery Walker. 'You stole it all.'

" 'Take care wot you're saying, Henery,' ses Bob Pretty, 'else I'll make you prove your words.'

" 'You stole my pig,' ses Herbert Smith.

" 'Oh, 'ave I?' ses Bob, reaching down a 'and o' pork. 'Is that your pig?' he ses.

" 'It's just about the size o' my pore pig,' ses Herbert Smith.

" 'Very usual size, I call it,' ses Bob Pretty; 'and them ducks and hins very usual-looking hins and ducks, I call 'em, except that they don't grow 'em so fat in these parts. It's a fine thing when a man's doing a honest bisness to 'ave these charges brought agin 'im. Dis-'eartening, I call it. I don't mind telling you that the tiger got in at my back winder the other night and took arf a pound o' sausage, but you don't 'ear me complaining and going about calling other people thieves.'

" 'Tiger be hanged,' ses Henery Walker, who was almost certain that a loin o' pork on the table was off 'is pig; 'you're the only tiger in these parts.'

"Why, Henery,' ses Bob Pretty, 'wot are you a-thinkin' of? Where's your memory? Why, it's on'y two or three days ago you see it and 'ad to get up a tree out of its way.'

"He smiled and shook 'is 'ead at 'im, but

Henery Walker on'y kept opening and shutting
'is mouth, and at last 'e went outside without
saying a word.

"'And Sam Jones see it, too,' ses Bob
Pretty; 'didn't you, Sam?'"

"Sam didn't answer 'im.

"'And Charlie Hall and Jack Minns and a
lot more,' ses Bob; 'besides, I see it myself.   I
can believe my own eyes, I s'pose?'"

"'We'll have the law on you,' ses Sam Jones.

"'As *you* like,' ses Bob Pretty; 'but I tell
you plain, I've got all the bills for this properly
made out, upstairs.   And there's pretty near a
dozen of you as'll 'ave to go in the box and
swear as you saw the tiger.   Now, can I sell
any of you a bit o' pork afore you go?   It's
delicious eating, and as soon as you taste it
you'll know it wasn't grown in Claybury.   Or
a pair o' ducks wot 'ave come from two 'undered miles off, and yet look as fresh as if they
was on'y killed last night.'"

"George Kettle, whose ducks 'ad gone the
night afore, went into the front room and
walked up and down fighting for 'is breath, but
it was all no good; nobody ever got the better

o' Bob Pretty. None of 'em could swear to their property, and even when it became known a month later that Bob Pretty and the tramp knew each other, nothing was done. But nobody ever 'eard any more of the tiger from that day to this."

A Mixed Proposal

A MIXED PROPOSAL

MAJOR BRILL, late of the Fenshire Volun-
unteers, stood in front of the small piece of
glass in the hatstand, and with a firm and
experienced hand gave his new silk hat a slight
tilt over the right eye. Then he took his cane
and a new pair of gloves, and with a military
but squeaky tread, passed out into the road.
It was a glorious day in early autumn, and the
soft English landscape was looking its best, but
despite the fact that there was nothing more
alarming in sight than a few cows on the hill-
side a mile away, the Major paused at his gate,
and his face took on an appearance of the
greatest courage and resolution before proceeding. The road was dusty and quiet, except for
the children playing at cottage doors, and so
hot that the Major, heedless of the fact that he
could not replace the hat at exactly the same

angle, stood in the shade of a tree while he removed it and mopped his heated brow.

He proceeded on his way more leisurely, overtaking, despite his lack of speed, another man who was walking still more slowly in the shade of the hedge.

"Fine day, Halibut," he said, briskly; "fine day."

"Beautiful," said the other, making no attempt to keep pace with him.

"Country wants rain, though," cried the Major over his shoulder.

Halibut assented, and walking slowly on, wondered vaguely what gaudy color it was that had attracted his eye. It dawned on him at length that it must be the Major's tie, and he suddenly quickened his pace, by no means reassured as the man of war also quickened his.

"Halloa, Brill!" he cried. "Half a moment."

The Major stopped and waited for his friend; Halibut eyed the tie uneasily—it was fearfully and wonderfully made—but said nothing.

"Well?" said the Major, somewhat sharply.

"Oh—I was going to ask you, Brill— Confound it! I've forgotten what I was going to say now. I daresay I shall soon think of it. You're not in a hurry?"

"Well, I am, rather," said Brill. "Fact is— Is my hat on straight, Halibut?"

The other assuring him that it was, the Major paused in his career, and gripping the brim with both hands, deliberately tilted it over the right eye again.

"You were saying—" said Halibut, regarding this manœuvre with secret disapproval.

"Yes," murmured the Major, "I was saying. Well, I don't mind telling an old friend like you, Halibut, though it is a profound secret. Makes me rather particular about my dress just now. Women notice these things. I'm— sha'nt get much sympathy from a confirmed old bachelor like you—but I'm on my way to put a very momentous question."

"The devil you are!" said the other, blankly.

"Sir!" said the astonished Major.

"Not Mrs. Riddel?" said Halibut.

"Certainly, sir," said the Major, stiffly. "Why not?"

"Only that I am going on the same errand," said the confirmed bachelor, with desperate calmness.

The Major looked at him, and for the first time noticed an unusual neatness and dressiness in his friend's attire.   His collar was higher than usual; his tie, of the whitest and finest silk, bore a pin he never remembered to have seen before; and for the first time since he had known him, the Major, with a strange sinking at the heart, saw that he wore spats.

"This is extraordinary," he said, briefly. "Well, good-day, Halibut.   Can't stop."

"Good-day," said the other.

The Major quickened his pace and shot ahead, and keeping in the shade of the hedge, ground his teeth as the civilian on the other side of the road slowly, but surely, gained on him.

It became exciting.   The Major was handicapped by his upright bearing and short military stride; the other, a simple child of the city, bent forward, swinging his arms and taking immense strides.   At a by-lane they picked up three small boys, who, trotting in their rear, made it evident by their remarks that they considered themselves the privileged spectators of a foot-race. The Major could stand it no longer, and with a cut of his cane at the foremost boy, softly called a halt.

"Well," said Halibut, stopping.

The man's manner was suspicious, not to say offensive, and the other had much ado to speak him fair.

"This is ridiculous," he said, trying to smile. "We can't walk in and propose in a duet. One of us must go to-day and the other to-morrow."

"Certainly," said Halibut; "that'll be the best plan."

"So childish,," said the Major, with a careless laugh, "two fellows walking in hot and tired and proposing to her."

"Absurd," replied Halibut, and both men eyed each other carefully.

"So, if I'm unsuccessful, old chap," said the Major, in a voice which he strove to render natural and easy, "I will come straight back to your place and let you know, so as not to keep you in suspense."

"You're very good," said Halibut, with some emotion; "but I think I'll take to-day, because I have every reason to believe that I have got one of my bilious attacks coming on to-morrow."

"Pooh! fancy, my dear fellow," said the Major, heartily; "I never saw you look better in my life."

"That's one of the chief signs," replied Halibut, shaking his head. "I'm afraid I must go to-day."

"I really cannot waive my right on account of your bilious attack," said the Major haughtily.

"Your *right?*" said Halibut, with spirit.

"My right!" repeated the other. "I should have been there before you if you had not stopped me in the first place."

"But I started first," said Halibut.

"Prove it," exclaimed the Major, warmly.

The other shrugged his shoulders.

"I shall certainly not give way," he said, calmly. "This is a matter in which my whole future is concerned. It seems very odd, not to say inconvenient, that you should have chosen the same day as myself, Brill, for such an errand—very odd."

"It's quite an accident," asseverated the Major; "as a matter of fact, Halibut, I nearly went yesterday. That alone gives me, I think, some claim to precedence."

"Just so," said Halibut, slowly; "it constitutes an excellent claim."

The Major regarded him with moistening eyes. This was generous and noble. His opinion of Halibut rose. "And now you have been so frank with me," said the latter, "it is only fair that you should know I started out with the same intention three days ago and found her out. So far as claims go, I think mine leads."

"Pure matter of opinion," said the disgusted Major; "it really seems as though we want an arbitrator. Well, we'll have to make our call together, I suppose, but I'll take care not to give you any opportunity, Halibut, so don't cherish any delusions on that point. Even *you* wouldn't have the hardihood to propose before a third party, I should think; but if you do, I give you fair warning that I shall begin, too."

"This is most unseemly," said Halibut. "We'd better both go home and leave it for another day."

"When do you propose going, then?" asked the Major.

"Really, I haven't made up my mind," replied the other.

The Major shrugged his shoulders.

"It won't do, Halibut," he said, grimly; "it won't do. I'm too old a soldier to be caught that way."

There was a long pause. The Major mopped his brow again. "I've got it," he said at last.

Halibut looked at him curiously.

"We must play for first proposal," said the Major, firmly. "We're pretty evenly matched."

"Chess?" gasped the other, a whole world of protest in his tones.

"Chess," repeated the Major.

"It is hardly respectful," demurred Halibut. "What do you think the lady would do if she heard of it?"

"Laugh," replied the Major, with conviction.

"I believe she would," said the other, brightening.   "I believe she would."

"You agree, then?"

"With conditions."

"Conditions?" repeated the Major.

"One game," said Halibut, speaking very slowly and distinctly; "and if the winner is refused, the loser not to propose until he gives him permission."

"What the deuce for?" inquired the other, suspiciously.

"Suppose I win," replied Halibut, with suspicious glibness, "and was so upset that I had one of my bilious attacks come on, where should I be?   Why, I might have to break off in the middle and go home.   A fellow can't propose when everything in the room is going round and round."

"I don't think you ought to contemplate marriage, Halibut," remarked the Major, very seriously and gently.

"Thanks," said Halibut, dryly.

"Very well," said the Major, "I agree to the conditions.   Better come to my place and we'll decide it now.   If we look sharp, the winner may be able to know his fate to-day, after all."

Halibut assenting, they walked back together. The feverish joy of the gambler showed in the Major's eye as they drew their chairs up to the little antique chess table and began to place their pieces ready for the fray. Then a thought struck him, and he crossed over to the sideboard.

"If you're feeling a bit off colour, Halibut," he said, kindly, "you'd better have a little brandy to pull yourself together. I don't wish to take a mean advantage."

"You're very good," said the other, as he eyed the noble measure of liquid poured out by his generous adversary.

"And now to business," said the Major, as he drew himself a little soda from a siphon.

"Now to business," repeated Halibut, rising and placing his glass on the mantel-piece.

The Major struggled fiercely with his feelings, but, despite himself, a guilty blush lent colour to the other's unfounded suspicions.

"Remember the conditions," said Halibut, impressively.

"Here's my hand on it," said the other, reaching over.

Halibut took it, and, his thoughts being at the moment far away, gave it a tender, respectful squeeze. The Major stared and coughed. It was suggestive of practice.

If the history of the duel is ever written, it will be found not unworthy of being reckoned with the most famous combats of ancient times. Piece after piece was removed from the board, and the Major drank glass after glass of soda to cool his heated brain. At the second glass Halibut took an empty tumbler and helped himself. Suddenly there was a singing in the Major's ears, and a voice, a hateful, triumphant voice, said,

"Checkmate!"

Then did his gaze wander from knight to bishop and bishop to castle in a vain search for succour. There was his king defied by a bishop —a bishop which had been hobnobbing with pawns in one corner of the board, and which he could have sworn he had captured and removed full twenty minutes before. He mentioned this impression to Halibut.

"That was the other one," said his foe. "I thought you had forgotten this. I have been watching and hoping so for the last half-hour."

There was no disguising the coarse satisfaction of the man. He had watched and hoped. Not beaten him, so the Major told himself, in fair play, but by taking a mean and pitiful advantage of a pure oversight. A sheer oversight. He admitted it.

Halibut rose with a sigh of relief, and the Major, mechanically sweeping up the pieces, dropped them one by one into the box.

"Plenty of time," said the victor, glancing at the clock. "I shall go now, but I should like a wash first."

The Major rose, and in his capacity of host led the way upstairs to his room, and poured fresh water for his foe. Halibut washed himself delicately, carefully trimming his hair and beard, and anxiously consulting the Major as to the set of his coat in the back, after he had donned it again.

His toilet completed, he gave a satisfied glance in the glass, and then followed the man of war sedately down stairs. At the hall he paused, and busied himself with the clothes-brush and hat-pad, modestly informing his glaring friend that he could not afford to throw any chances away, and then took his departure.

The Major sat up late that night waiting for news, but none came, and by breakfast-time next morning his thirst for information became almost uncontrollable. He toyed with a chop and allowed his coffee to get cold. Then he clapped on his hat and set off to Halibut's to know the worst.

"Well?" he inquired, as he followed the other into his dining-room.

"I went," said Halibut, waving him to a chair.

"Am I to congratulate you?"

"Well, I don't know," was the reply; "perhaps not just yet."

"What do you mean by that?" said the Major, irascibly.

"Well, as a matter of fact," said Halibut, "she refused me, but so nicely and so gently that I scarcely minded it. In fact, at first I hardly realized that she had refused me."

The Major rose, and regarding his poor friend kindly, shook and patted him lightly on the shoulder.

"She's a splendid woman," said Halibut.

"Ornament to her sex," remarked the Major.

"So considerate," murmured the bereaved one.

"Good women always are," said the Major, decisively. "I don't think I'd better worry her to-day, Halibut, do you?"

"No, I don't," said Halibut, stiffly.

"I'll try my luck to-morrow," said the Major.

"I beg your pardon," said Halibut.

"Eh?" said the Major, trying to look puzzled.

"You are forgetting the conditions of the game," replied Halibut. "You have to obtain my permission first."

"Why, my dear fellow," said the Major, with a boisterous laugh. "I wouldn't insult you by questioning your generosity in such a case. No, no, Halibut, old fellow, I know you too well."

He spoke with feeling, but there was an anxious note in his voice.

"We must abide by the conditions," said Halibut, slowly; "and I must inform you, Brill, that I intend to renew the attack myself."

"Then, sir," said the Major, fuming, "you compel me to say—putting all modesty aside—that I believe the reason Mrs. Riddel would have nothing to do with you was because she thought *somebody else* might make a similar offer."

"That's what I thought," said Halibut, simply; "but you see now that you have so unaccountably—so far as Mrs. Riddel is concerned—dropped out of the running, perhaps, if I am gently persistent, she'll take me."

The Major rose and glared at him.

"If you don't take care, old chap," said Halibut, tenderly, "you'll burst something."

"Gently persistent," repeated the Major, staring at him; "gently persistent."

"Remember Bruce and his spider," smiled the other.

"You are *not* going to propose to that

poor woman nine times?" roared his incensed friend.

"I hope that it will not be necessary," was the reply; "but if it is, I can assure you, my dear Brill, that I'm not going to be outclassed by a mere spider."

"But think of her feelings!" gasped the Major.

"I have," was the reply; "and I'm sure she'll thank me for it afterward. You see, Brill, you and I are the only eligibles in the place, and now you are out of it, she's sure to take me sooner or later."

"And pray how long am I to wait?" demanded the Major, controlling himself with difficulty.

"I can't say," said Halibut; "but I don't think it's any good your waiting at all, because if I see any signs that Mrs. Riddel is waiting for you I may just give her a hint of the hopelessness of it."

"You're a perfect Mephistopheles, sir!" bawled the indignant Major.

Halibut bowed.

"Strategy, my dear Brill," he said, smiling; "strategy. Now why waste your time? Why not make some other woman happy? Why not try her companion, Miss Philpotts? I'm sure any little assistance——"

The Major's attitude was so alarming that the sentence was never finished, and a second later the speaker found himself alone, watching his irate friend hurrying frantically down the path, knocking the blooms off the geraniums with his cane as he went. He saw no more of him for several weeks, the Major preferring to cherish his resentment in the privacy of his house. The Major also refrained from seeing the widow, having a wholesome dread as to what effect the contemplation of her charms might have upon his plighted word.

He met her at last by chance. Mrs. Riddel bowed coldly and would have passed on, but the Major had already stopped, and was making wild and unmerited statements about the weather.

"It is seasonable," she said, simply.

The Major agreed with her, and with a strong.effort regained his composure.

"I was just going to turn back," he said, untruthfully; "may I walk with you?"

"I am not going far," was the reply.

With soldierly courage the Major took this as permission; with feminine precision Mrs. Riddel walked about fifty yards and then stopped. "I told you I wasn't going far," she said sweetly, as she held out her hand. "Goodby."

"I wanted to ask you something," said the Major, turning with her. "I can't think what it was.

They walked on very slowly, the Major's heart beating rapidly as he told himself that the lady's coldness was due to his neglect of the past few weeks, and his wrath against Halibut rose to still greater heights as he saw the cruel position in which that schemer had placed him. Then he made a sudden resolution. There was no condition as to secrecy, and, first turning the conversation on to indoor amusements, he told the astonished Mrs. Riddel the full particulars of the fatal game. Mrs. Riddel said that she would never forgive them; it was the most preposterous thing she had ever heard of. And she demanded hotly whether she was to spend the rest of her life in refusing Mr. Halibut.

"Do you play high as a rule?" she inquired, scornfully.

"Sixpence a game," replied the Major, simply.

The corners of Mrs. Riddel's mouth relaxed, and her fine eyes began to water; then she turned her head away and laughed. "It was very foolish of us, I admit," said the Major, ruefully, "and very wrong. I shouldn't have told you, only I couldn't explain my apparent neglect without."

"Apparent neglect?" repeated the widow, somewhat haughtily.

"Well, put it down to a guilty conscience," said the Major; "it seems years to me since I have seen you."

"Remember the conditions, Major Brill," said Mrs. Riddel, with severity.

"I shall not transgress them," replied the Major, seriously.

Mrs. Riddel gave her head a toss, and regarded him from the corner of her eyes.

"I am very angry with you, indeed," she said, severely. The Major apologized again. "For losing," added the lady, looking straight before her.

Major Brill caught his breath and his knees trembled beneath him. He made a half-hearted attempt to seize her hand, and then remembering his position, sighed deeply and looked straight before him. They walked on in silence.

"I think," said his companion at last, "that, if you like, you can get back at cribbage what you lost at chess. That is, of course, if you really want to."

"He wouldn't play," said the Major, shaking his head.

"No, but I will," said Mrs. Riddel, with a smile. "I think I've got a plan."

She blushed charmingly, and then, in modest alarm at her boldness, dropped her voice almost to a whisper. The Major gazed at her in speechless admiration and threw back his head in ecstasy. "Come round to-morrow afternoon," said Mrs. Riddel, pausing at the end of the lane. "Mr. Halibut shall be there, too, and it shall be done under his very eyes."

Until that time came the Major sat at home carefully rehearsing his part, and it was with an air of complacent virtue that he met the somewhat astonished gaze of the persistent Halibut next day. It was a bright afternoon, but they sat indoors, and Mrs. Riddel, after an animated description of a game at cribbage with Miss Philpotts the night before, got the cards out and challenged Halibut to a game.

They played two, both of which the diplomatic Halibut lost; then Mrs. Riddel, dismissing him as incompetent, sat drumming on the table with her fingers, and at length challenged the Major. She lost the first game easily, and began the second badly. Finally, after hastily glancing at a new hand, she flung the cards petulantly on the table, face downward.

"Would you like my hand, Major Brill?" she demanded, with a blush.

"Better than anything in the world," cried the Major, eagerly.

Halibut started, and Miss Philpotts nearly had an accident with her crochet hook. The only person who kept cool was Mrs. Riddel, and it was quite clear to the beholders that she had realized neither the ambiguity of her question nor the meaning of her opponent's reply.

"Well, you may have it," she said, brightly.

Before Miss Philpotts could lay down her work, before Mr. Halibut could interpose, the Major took possession of Mrs. Riddel's small white hand and raised it gallantly to his lips. Mrs. Riddel, with a faint scream which was a perfect revelation to the companion, snatched her hand away. "I meant my hand of cards," she said, breathlessly.

"Really, Brill, really," said Halibut, stepping forward fussily.

"Oh!" said the Major, blankly; "cards!"

"That's what I meant, of course," said Mrs. Riddel, recovering herself with a laugh. "I had no idea——still—if you prefer——" The Major took her hand again, and Miss Philpotts set Mr. Halibut an example—which he did not follow—by gazing meditatively out of the window. Finally she gathered up her work and quitted the room. Mrs. Riddel smiled over at Mr. Halibut and nodded toward the Major.

"DON'T YOU THINK MAJOR BRILL IS SOMEWHAT HASTY
IN HIS CONCLUSIONS?" SHE INQUIRED SOFTLY.

"Don't you think Major Brill is somewhat hasty in his conclusions?" she inquired, softly.

"I'll tell Major Brill what I think of him when I get him alone," said the injured gentleman, sourly.

An Adulteration Act

AN ADULTERATION ACT

DR. FRANK CARSON had been dreaming tantalizing dreams of cooling, effervescent beverages. Over and over again in his dreams he had risen from his bed, and tripping lightly down to the surgery in his pajamas, mixed himself something long and cool and fizzy, without being able to bring the dream to a satisfactory termination.

With a sudden start he awoke. The thirst was still upon him; the materials for quenching it, just down one flight of stairs. He would have smacked his lips at the prospect if they had been moist enough to smack; as it was, he pushed down the bedclothes, and throwing one leg out of bed—became firmly convinced that he was still dreaming.

For the atmosphere was stifling and odorous, and the ceiling descended in an odd bulg-

ing curve to within a couple of feet of his head.
Still half asleep, he raised his fist and prodded
at it in astonishment—a feeling which gave
way to one of stupefaction as the ceiling took
another shape and swore distinctly.

"I *must* be dreaming," mused the doctor;
"even the ceiling seems alive."

He prodded it again—regarding it closely
this time.　The ceiling at once rose to greater
altitudes, and at the same moment an old face
with bushy whiskers crawled under the edge of
it, and asked him profanely what he meant by
it.　It also asked him whether he wanted something for himself, because, if so, he was going
the right way to work.

"Where am I?" demanded the bewildered
doctor.　*"Mary!　Mary!"*

He started up in bed, and brought his head
in sudden violent contact with the ceiling.
Then, before the indignant ceiling could carry
out its threat of a moment before, he slipped
out of bed and stood on a floor which was in its
place one moment and somewhere else the next.

In the smell of bilge-water, tar, and the fœtid
atmosphere generally his clouded brain awoke

to the fact that he was on board ship, but resolutely declined to inform him how he got there. He looked down in disgust at the ragged clothes which he had on in lieu of the usual pajamas; and then, as events slowly pieced themselves together in his mind, remembered, as the last thing that he could remember, that he had warned his friend Harry Thomson, solicitor, that if he had any more to drink it would not be good for him.

He wondered dimly as he stood whether Thomson was there too, and walking unsteadily round the forecastle, roused the sleepers, one by one, and asked them whether they were Harry Thomson, all answering with much fluency in the negative, until he came to one man who for some time made no answer at all.

The doctor shook him first and then punched him. Then he shook him again and gave him little scientific slaps, until at length Harry Thomson, in a far-away voice, said that he was all right.

"Well, I'm glad I'm not alone," said the doctor, selfishly. *"Harry! Harry! Wake up!"*

"All ri'!" said the sleeper; "I'm all ri'!"

The doctor shook him again, and then rolled him backward and forward in his bunk. Under this gentle treatment the solicitor's faculties were somewhat brightened, and, half opening his eyes, he punched viciously at the disturber of his peace, until threatening voices from the gloom promised to murder both of them.

"Where are we?" demanded the doctor, of a deep voice from the other side of the forecastle which had been particularly threatening.

"Barque *Stella,* o' course," was the reply. "Where'd you think you was?"

The doctor gripped the edge of his friend's bunk and tried to think; then, a feeling of nausea overcoming all others, he clambered hurriedly up the forecastle ladder and lurched to the side of the vessel.

He leaned there for some time without moving, a light breeze cooling his fevered brow, and a small schooner some little distance from them playing seesaw, as he closed his eyes to the heaving blue sea. Land was conspicuous by its absence, and with a groan he turned and looked about him—at the white scrubbed deck, the snowy canvas towering aloft on lazily creaking spars, and the steersman leaning against the wheel regarding the officer who stood near by.

Dr. Carson, feeling a little better, walked sternly aft, the officer turning round and glancing in surprise at his rags as he approached.

"I beg your pardon," began the doctor, in superior tones.

"And what the devil do you want?" demanded the second officer; "who told you to come along here?"

"I want to know what this means," said the doctor, fiercely. "How dare you kidnap us on your beastly bilge-tank?"

"Man's mad," murmured the astonished second officer.

"Insufferable outrage!" continued the doctor. "Take us back to Melbourne at once."

"You get for'ard," said the other sharply; "get for'ard, and don't let me have any more of your lip."

"I want to see the captain of this ship," cried the doctor; "go and fetch him at once."

The second officer gazed at him, limp with

astonishment, and then turned to the steersman, as though unable to believe his ears. The steersman pointed in front of him, and the other gave a cry of surprise and rage as he saw another tatterdemalion coming with uncertain steps toward him.

"Carson," said the new arrival, feebly; and coming closer to his friend, clung to him miserably.

"I'm just having it out with 'em, Thomson," said the doctor, energetically. "My friend here is a solicitor. Tell him what 'll happen if they don't take us back, Harry."

"You seem to be unaware, my good fellow," said the solicitor, covering a large hole in the leg of his trousers with his hand, "of the very dangerous situation in which you have placed yourselves. We have no desire to be harsh with you——"

"Not at all," acquiesced the doctor, nodding at the second officer.

"At the same time," continued Mr. Thomson—"at the——" He let go his friend's arm and staggered away; the doctor gazed after him sympathetically.

HE SAW ANOTHER TATTERDEMALION COMING TOWARDS HIM.

"His digestion is not all it should be," he said to the second officer, confidentially.

"If you don't get for'ard in two twos," said that gentleman, explosively, "I'll knock your heads off."

The doctor gazed at him in haughty disdain, and taking the limp Thomson by the arm, led him slowly away.

"How did we get here?" asked Mr. Harry Thomson, feebly.

The doctor shook his head.

"How did we get these disgusting clothes on?" continued his friend.

The doctor shook his head again. "The last thing I can remember, Harry," he said, slowly, "was imploring you not to drink any more."

"I didn't hear you," said the solicitor, crustily; "your speech was very indistinct last night."

"Seemed so to you, I dare say," said the other.

Mr. Thomson shook his arm off, and clinging to the mainmast, leaned his cheek against it and closed his eyes. He opened them again at the sound of voices, and drew himself up as he saw the second officer coming along with a stern-visaged man of about fifty.

"Are you the master of this vessel?" inquired the doctor, stepping to his friend's side.

"What the blazes has that got to do with you?" demanded the skipper. "Look here, my lads; don't you play any of your little games on me, because they won't do. You're both of you as drunk as owls."

"Defamation of character," said the solicitor, feebly, to his friend.

"Allow me," said the doctor, with his best manner, "to inquire what all this means. I am Dr. Frank Carson, of Melbourne; this gentleman is my friend Mr. Thomson, of the same place, solicitor."

"*What?*" roared the skipper, the veins in his forehead standing out. "Doctor! Solicitor! Why, you damned rascals, you shipped with me as cook and A. B."

"There's some mistake," said the doctor. "I'm afraid I shall have to ask you to take us back. I hope you haven't come far."

"Take those scarecrows away," cried the

skipper, hoarsely; "take them away before I do them a mischief. I'll have the law of somebody for shipping two useless lubbers as seamen. Look to me like pickpockets."

"You shall answer for this," said Carson, foaming; "we're professional men, and we're not going to be abused by a bargee."

"Let him talk," said Mr. Thomson, hurriedly drawing his friend away from the irate skipper. "Let him talk."

"I'll put you both in quod when we get to Hong-kong," said the skipper. "Meantime, no work, no food; d'ye hear? Start and cook the breakfast, Mr. Doctor; and you, Mr. Lawyer, turn to and ask the boy to teach you an A. B's duties."

He walked back to the cabin; and the new cook was slowly pushed toward the galley by the second officer, the new A. B., under the same gentle guidance, being conducted back to the forecastle.

Fortunately for the new seamen the weather continued fine, but the heat of the galley was declared by the new cook to be insupportable. From the other hands they learned that they had been shipped with several others by a resourceful boarding-house master. The other hands, being men of plain speech, also said that they were brought aboard in a state of beastly and enviable intoxication, and chaffed crudely when the doctor attributed their apparent state of intoxication to drugs.

"You say you're a doctor?" said the oldest seaman.

"I am," said Carson, fiercely.

"Wot sort of a doctor are you, if you don't know when your licker's been played with, then?" asked the old man, as a grin passed slowly from mouth to mouth.

"I suppose it is because I drink so seldom," said the doctor, loftily. "I hardly know the taste of liquor myself, while as for my friend Mr. Thomson, you might almost call him a tee-totaler.

"Next door to one," said the solicitor, who was sewing a patch on his trousers, as he looked up approvingly.

"You *might* call 'im a sailor, if you liked," said another seaman, "but that wouldn't make him one. All I can say is I never 'ad enough

"YOU SAY YOU'RE A DOCTOR?"

time or money to get in the state you was both in when you come aboard."

If the forecastle was incredulous, the cabin was worse. The officers at first took but little notice of them, but feeling their torn and tattered appearance was against them, they put on so many airs and graces to counteract this that flesh and blood could not endure it quietly. The cook would allude to his friend as Mr. Thomson, while the A. B. would persist in referring, with a most affected utterance, to Dr. Carson.

"Cook!" bawled the skipper one day when they were about a week out.

Dr. Carson, who was peeling potatoes, stepped slowly out of the galley and went toward him.

"You say 'Sir,' when you're spoken to," said the skipper, fiercely.

The doctor sneered.

"My—if you sneer at me, I'll knock your head off!" said the other, with a wicked look.

"When you get back to Melbourne," said the doctor, quietly, "you'll hear more of this."

"You're a couple of pickpockets aping the

gentleman," said the skipper, and he turned to the mate.   "Mr. Mackenzie, what do these two ragamuffins look like?"

"Pickpockets," said the mate, dutifully.

"It's a very handy thing," said the old man, jeeringly, "to have a doctor aboard.   First time I've carried a surgeon."

Mr. Mackenzie guffawed loudly.

"And a solicitor," said the skipper, gazing darkly at the hapless Harry Thomson, who was cleaning brasswork.   "Handy in case of disputes.   He's a real sea lawyer.   *Cook!*"

"Sir?" said the doctor, quietly.

"Go down and tidy my cabin, and see you do it well."

The doctor went below without a word, and worked like a housemaid.   When he came on deck again, his face wore a smile almost of happiness, and his hand caressed one trousers pocket as though it concealed a hidden weapon.

For the following three or four days the two unfortunates were worked unceasingly.   Mr. Thomson complained bitterly, but the cook wore a sphinxlike smile and tried to comfort him.

"It won't be for long, Harry," he said, consolingly.

The solicitor sniffed. "I could write tract after tract on temperance," he said, bitterly. "I wonder what our poor wives are thinking? I expect they have put us down as dead."

"Crying their eyes out," said the doctor, wistfully; "but they'll dry them precious quick when we get back, and ask all sorts of questions. What are you going to say, Harry?"

"The truth," said the solicitor, virtuously.

"So am I," said his friend; "but mind, we must both tell the same tale, whatever it is. Halloa! what's the matter?"

"It's the skipper," said the boy, who had just run up; "he wants to see you at once. He's dying."

He caught hold of the doctor by the sleeve; but Carson, in his most professional manner, declined to be hurried. He went leisurely down the companion-ladder, and met with a careless glance the concerned faces of the mate and second officer.

"Come to the skipper at once," said the mate.

"Does he want to see me?" said the doctor, languidly, as he entered the cabin.

The skipper was lying doubled up in his bunk, his face twisted with pain. "Doctor," he panted, "give me something quick. There's the medicine-chest."

"Do you want some food, sir?" inquired the other, respectfully.

"Food be damned!" said the sufferer. "I want physic. There's the medicine-chest."

The doctor took it up and held it out to him.

"I don't want the lot," moaned the skipper. "I want you to give me something for red-hot corkscrews in the inside."

"I beg your pardon," said the doctor, humbly; "I'm only the cook."

"If you—don't—prescribe for me at once," said the skipper, "I'll put you in irons."

The doctor shook his head. "I shipped as cook," he said, slowly.

"Give me something, for Heaven's sake!" said the skipper, humbly. "I'm dying."

The doctor pondered.

"If you dinna treat him at once, I'll break your skull," said the mate, persuasively.

The doctor regarded him scornfully, and turned to the writhing skipper.

"My fee is half a guinea a visit," he said, softly; "five shillings if you come to me."

"I'll have half a guinea's worth," said the agonized skipper.

The doctor took his wrist, and calmly drew the second officer's watch from its owner's pocket. Then he inspected the sick man's tongue, and shaking his head, selected a powder from the chest.

"You mustn't mind its being nasty," he said. "Where's a spoon?"

He looked round for one, but the skipper took the powder from his hand, and licked it from the paper as though it had been sherbet.

"For mercy's sake don't say it's cholera," he gasped.

"I won't say anything," said the doctor. "Where did you say the money was?"

The skipper pointed to his trousers, and Mr. Mackenzie, his national spirit rising in hot rage, took out the agreed amount and handed it to the physician.

"Am I in danger?" said the skipper.

"There's always danger," said the doctor, in his best bedside manner. "Have you made your will?"

The other, turning pale, shook his head.

"Perhaps you'd like to see a solicitor?" said Carson, in winning tones.

"I'm not bad enough for that," said the skipper, stoutly.

"You must stay here and nurse the skipper, Mr. Mackenzie," said Carson, turning to the mate; "and be good enough not to make that snuffling noise; it's worrying to an invalid."

"Snuffling noise?" repeated the horror-struck mate.

"Yes; you've got an unpleasant habit of snuffling," said the doctor; "it worries me sometimes. I meant to speak to you about it before. You mustn't do it here. If you want to snuffle, go and snuffle on deck."

The frenzied outburst of the mate was interrupted by the skipper. "Don't make that noise in my cabin, Mr. Mackenzie," he said, severely.

Both mates withdrew in dudgeon, and Carson, after arranging the sufferer's bedclothes, quitted the cabin and sought his friend. Mr.

Thomson was at first incredulous, but his eyes glistened brightly at the sight of the half-sovereign.

"Better hide it," he said, apprehensively; "the skipper 'll have it back when he gets well; it's the only coin we've got."

"He won't get well," said Dr. Carson, easily; "not till we get to Hong-kong, that is."

"What's the matter with him?" whispered the solicitor.

The doctor, evading his eye, pulled a long face and shook his head. "It may be the cooking," he said, slowly. "I'm not a good cook, I admit. It might be something got into the food from the medicine-chest. I shouldn't be at all surprised if the mates are taken bad too."

And indeed at that very moment the boy came rushing to the galley again, bawling out that Mr. Mackenzie was lying flat on his stomach in his bunk, punching the air with his fists and rending it with his language. The second officer appeared on deck as he finished his tale, and glancing forward, called out loudly for the cook.

"You're wanted, Frank," said the solicitor.

"When he calls me doctor, I'll go," said the other, stiffly.

"*Cook!*" bawled the second officer. "*Cook!* Cook!"

He came running forward, his face red and angry, and his fist doubled. "Didn't you hear me calling you?" he demanded, fiercely.

"I've been promoted," said Carson, sweetly. "I'm ship's surgeon now."

"Come down below at once, or I'll take you there by the scruff of your neck," vociferated the other.

"You're not big enough, little man," said the doctor, still smiling. "Well, well, lead the way, and we'll see what we can do."

He followed the speechless second officer below, and found the boy's description of the first officer's state as moonlight unto sunlight, as water unto wine. Even the second officer was appalled at the spectacle, and ventured a protest.

"Gie me something at once," yelled Mr. Mackenzie.

"Do you wish me to undertake your case?" inquired the doctor, suavely.

Mr. Mackenzie said that he did, in seven long, abusive, and wicked sentences.

"My fee is half a guinea," said the doctor, softly, poor people who cannot afford more, mates and the like, I sometimes treat for less."

"I'll die first," howled the mate; "you won't get any money out of me."

"Very good," said the doctor, and rose to depart.

"Bring him back, Rogers," yelled the mate; "don't let him go."

But the second officer, with a strange awesome look in his eyes, was leaning back in his seat, tightly gripping the edge of the table in both hands.

"Come, come," said the doctor, cheerily; "what's this? You mustn't be ill, Rogers. I want you to nurse these other two."

The other rose slowly to his feet and eyed him with lack-lustre eyes. "Tell the third officer to take charge," he said, slowly; "and if he's to be nurse as well, he's got his hands full."

The doctor sent the boy to apprise the third officer of his responsibilities, and then stood watching the extraordinary and snakelike convolutions of Mr. Mackenzie.

"How much—did—ye say?" hissed the latter.

"Poor people," repeated the doctor, with relish, "five shillings a visit; very poor people, half a crown."

"I'll have half a crown's worth," moaned the miserable mate.

"Mr. Mackenzie," said a faint voice from the skipper's cabin.

"Sir?" yelled the mate, who was in torment.

"Don't answer me like that, sir," said the skipper, sharply. "Will you please to remember that I'm ill, and can't bear that horrible noise you're making?"

"I'm—ill—too," gasped the mate.

"Ill? Nonsense!" said the skipper, severely. "We can't both be ill. How about the ship?"

There was no reply, but from another cabin the voice of Mr. Rogers was heard calling wildly for medical aid, and offering impossible sums in exchange for it. The doctor went from cabin to cabin, and, first collecting his fees, administered sundry potions to the sufferers; and then, in his capacity of cook, went forward and made an unsavory mess he called gruel, which he insisted upon their eating.

Thanks to his skill, the invalids were freed from the more violent of their pains, but this freedom was followed by a weakness so alarming that they could hardly raise their heads from their pillows—a state of things which excited the intense envy of the third officer, who, owing to his responsibilities, might just as well have been without one.

In this state of weakness, and with the fear of impending dissolution before his eyes, the skipper sent for Mr. Harry Thomson, and after some comparisons between lawyers and sharks, in which stress was laid upon certain redeeming features of the latter, paid a guinea and made his will. His example, save in the amount of the fee, was followed by the mate; but Mr. Rogers, being approached tentatively by the doctor in his friend's behalf, shook his head and thanked his stars he had nothing to leave. He had enjoyed his money, he said.

They mended slowly as they approached

Hong-kong, though a fit of temper on Mr. Mackenzie's part, during which he threw out ominous hints about having his money back, led to a regrettable relapse in his case. He was still in bed when they came to anchor in the harbour; but the skipper and his second officer were able to go above and exchange congratulations from adjoining deck-chairs.

"You are sure it wasn't cholera?" asked the harbour-master's deputy, who had boarded them in his launch, after he had heard the story.

"Positive," said Carson.

"Very fortunate thing they had you on board," said the deputy—"very fortunate."

The doctor bowed.

"Seems so odd, the three of them being down with it," said the other; "looks as though it's infectious, doesn't it?"

"I don't think so," said the doctor, accepting with alacrity an offer to go ashore in the launch and change into some decent clothes. "I think I know what it was."

The captain of the *Stella* pricked up his ears, and the second officer leaned forward with parted lips. Carson, accompanied by the

THE SECOND OFFICER LEANED FORWARD.

deputy and the solicitor, walked toward the launch.

"What was it?" cried the skipper, anxiously.

"I think that you ate something that disagreed with you," replied the doctor, grinning meaningly. "Good-by, captain."

The master of the *Stella* made no reply, but rising feebly, tottered to the side, and shook his fist at the launch as it headed for the shore. Doctor Carson, who had had a pious upbringing, kissed his hand in return.

A Golden Venture

A GOLDEN VENTURE

THE elders of the Tidger family sat at breakfast—Mrs. Tidger with knees wide apart and the youngest Tidger nestling in the valley of print-dress which lay between, and Mr. Tidger bearing on one moleskin knee a small copy of himself in a red flannel frock and a slipper. The larger Tidger children took the solids of their breakfast up and down the stone-flagged court outside, coming in occasionally to gulp draughts of very weak tea from a gallipot or two which stood on the table, and to wheedle Mr. Tidger out of any small piece of bloater which he felt generous enough to bestow.

"Peg away, Ann," said Mr. Tidger, heartily.

His wife's elder sister shook her head, and passing the remains of her slice to one of her small nephews, leaned back in her chair. "No appetite, Tidger," she said, slowly.

"You should go in for carpentering," said Mr. Tidger, in justification of the huge crust he was carving into mouthfuls with his pocket-knife. "Seems to me I can't eat enough sometimes. Hullo, who's the letter for?"

He took it from the postman, who stood at the door amid a bevy of Tidgers who had followed him up the court, and slowly read the address.

" 'Mrs. Ann Pullen,' " he said, handing it over to his sister-in-law; "nice writing, too."

Mrs. Pullen broke the envelope, and after a somewhat lengthy search for her pocket, fumbled therein for her spectacles. She then searched the mantelpiece, the chest of drawers, and the dresser, and finally ran them to earth on the copper.

She was not a good scholar, and it took her some time to read the letter, a proceeding which she punctuated with such "Ohs" and "Ahs" and gaspings and "God bless my souls" as nearly drove the carpenter and his wife, who were leaning forward impatiently, to the verge of desperation.

"Who's it from?" asked Mr. Tidger for the third time.

"I don't know," said Mrs. Pullen. "Good gracious, who ever would ha' thought it!"

"Thought what, Ann?" demanded the carpenter, feverishly.

"Why don't people write their names plain?" demanded his sister-in-law, impatiently. "It's got a printed name up in the corner; perhaps that's it. Well, I never did—I don't know whether I'm standing on my head or my heels."

"You're sitting down, that's what you're a-doing," said the carpenter, regarding her somewhat unfavourably.

"Perhaps it's a take-in," said Mrs. Pullen, her lips trembling. "I've heard o' such things. If it is, I shall never get over it—never."

"Get—over—what?" asked the carpenter.

"It don't look like a take-in," soliloquized Mrs. Pullen, "and I shouldn't think anybody'd go to all that trouble and spend a penny to take in a poor thing like me."

Mr. Tidger, throwing politeness to the winds, leaped forward, and snatching the letter from her, read it with feverish haste, tempered by a defective education.

"It's a take-in, Ann," he said, his voice trembling; "it must be."

"What is?" asked Mrs. Tidger, impatiently.

"Looks like it," said Mrs. Pullen, feebly.

"What is it?" screamed Mrs. Tidger, wrought beyond all endurance.

Her husband turned and regarded her with much severity, but Mrs. Tidger's gaze was the stronger, and after a vain attempt to meet it, he handed her the letter.

Mrs. Tidger read it through hastily, and then snatching the baby from her lap, held it out with both arms to her husband, and jumping up, kissed her sister heartily, patting her on the back in her excitement until she coughed with the pain of it.

"You don't think it's a take-in, Polly?" she inquired.

"Take-in?" said her sister; "of course it ain't. Lawyers don't play jokes; their time's too valuable. No, you're an heiress all right, Ann, and I wish you joy. I couldn't be more pleased if it was myself."

She kissed her again, and going to pat her back once more, discovered that she had sunk down sufficiently low in her chair to obtain the protection of its back.

"Two thousand pounds," said Mrs. Pullen, in an awestruck voice.

"Ten hundered pounds twice over," said the carpenter, mouthing it slowly; "twenty hundered pounds."

He got up from the table, and instinctively realizing that he could not do full justice to his feelings with the baby in his arms, laid it on the teatray in a puddle of cold tea and stood looking hard at the heiress.

"I was housekeeper to her eleven years ago," said Mrs. Pullen.   "I wonder what she left it to me for?"

"Didn't know what to do with it, I should think," said the carpenter, still staring openmouthed.

"Tidger, I'm ashamed of you," said his wife, snatching her infant to her bosom.   "I expect you was very good to her, Ann."

"I never 'ad no luck," said the impenitent carpenter.   "Nobody ever left me no money.

Nobody ever left me so much as a fi-pun note."

He stared round disdainfully at his poor belongings, and drawing on his coat, took his bag from a corner, and hoisting it on his shoulder, started to his work. He scattered the news as he went, and it ran up and down the little main street of Thatcham, and thence to the outlying lanes and cottages. Within a couple of hours it was common property, and the fortunate legatee was presented with a congratulatory address every time she ventured near the door.

It is an old adage that money makes friends; the carpenter was surprised to find that the mere fact of his having a moneyed relation had the same effect, and that men to whom he had hitherto shown a certain amount of respect due to their position now sought his company. They stood him beer at the "Bell," and walked by his side through the street. When they took to dropping in of an evening to smoke a pipe the carpenter was radiant with happiness.

"You don't seem to see beyond the end of your nose, Tidger," said the wife of his bosom after they had retired one evening.

"H'm?" said the startled carpenter.

"What do you think old Miller, the dealer, comes here for?" demanded his wife.

"Smoke his pipe," replied her husband, confidently.

"And old Wiggett?" persisted Mrs. Tidger.

"Smoke *his* pipe," was the reply. "Why, what's the matter, Polly?"

Mrs. Tidger sniffed derisively. "You men are all alike," she snapped. "What do you think Ann wears that pink bodice for?"

"I never noticed she 'ad a pink bodice, Polly," said the carpenter.

"No? That's what I say. You men never notice anything," said his wife. "If you don't send them two old fools off, I will."

"Don't you like 'em to see Ann wearing pink?" inquired the mystified Tidger.

Mrs. Tidger bit her lip and shook her head at him scornfully. "In plain English, Tidger, as plain as I can speak it," she said, severely, "they're after Ann and 'er bit o' money."

Mr. Tidger gazed at her open-mouthed, and taking advantage of that fact, blew out the candle to hide his discomposure.   "What!" he said, blankly, "at 'er time o' life?"

"Watch 'em to-morrer," said his wife.

The carpenter acted upon his instructions, and his ire rose as he noticed the assiduous attention paid by his two friends to the frivolous Mrs. Pullen.   Mr. Wiggett, a sharp-featured little man, was doing most of the talking, while his rival, a stout, clean-shaven man with a slow, oxlike eye, looked on stolidly.   Mr. Miller was seldom in a hurry, and lost many a bargain through his slowness—a fact which sometimes so painfully affected the individual who had outdistanced him that he would offer to let him have it at a still lower figure.

"You get younger than ever, Mrs. Pullen," said Wiggett, the conversation having turned upon ages.

"Young ain't the word for it," said Miller, with a praiseworthy determination not to be left behind.

"No; it's age as you're thinking of, Mr. Wiggett," said the carpenter, slowly; "none of us gets younger, do we, Ann?"

"YOU GET YOUNGER THAN EVER, MRS. PULLEN."

"Some of us keeps young in our ways," said Mrs. Pullen, somewhat shortly.

"How old should you say Ann is now?" persisted the watchful Tidger.

Mr. Wiggett shook his head. "I should say she's about fifteen years younger nor me," he said, slowly, "and I'm as lively as a cricket."

"She's fifty-five," said the carpenter.

"That makes you seventy, Wiggett," said Mr. Miller, pointedly. "I thought you was more than that. You look it."

Mr. Wiggett coughed sourly. "I'm fifty-nine," he growled. "Nothing 'll make me believe as Mrs. Pullen's fifty-five, nor anywhere near it."

"Ho!" said the carpenter, on his mettle— "ho! Why, my wife here was the sixth child, and she—— He caught a gleam in the sixth child's eye, and expressed her age with a cough. The others waited politely until he had finished, and Mr. Tidger, noticing this, coughed again.

"And she——" prompted Mr. Miller, displaying a polite interest.

"She ain't so young as she was," said the carpenter.

"Cares of a family," said Mr. Wiggett, plumping boldly. "I always thought Mrs. Pullen was younger than her."

"So did I," said Mr. Miller, "much younger."

Mr. Wiggett eyed him sharply. It was rather hard to have Miller hiding his lack of invention by participating in his compliments and even improving upon them. It was the way he dealt at market—listening to other dealers' accounts of their wares, and adding to them for his own.

"I was noticing you the other day, ma'am," continued Mr. Wiggett. "I see you going up the road with a step free and easy as a young girl's."

"She allus walks like that," said Mr. Miller, in a tone of surprised reproof.

"It's in the family," said the carpenter, who had been uneasily watching his wife's face.

"Both of you seem to notice a lot," said Mrs. Tidger; "much more than you used to."

Mr. Tidger, who was of a nervous and sensitive disposition, coughed again.

"You ought to take something for that cough," said Mr. Wiggett, considerately.

"Gin and beer," said Mr. Miller, with the air of a specialist.

"Bed's the best thing for it," said Mrs. Tidger, whose temper was beginning to show signs of getting out of hand.

Mr. Tidger rose and looked awkwardly at his visitors; Mr. Wiggett got up, and pretending to notice the time, said he must be going, and looked at Mr. Miller. That gentleman, who was apparently deep in some knotty problem, was gazing at the floor, and oblivious for the time to his surroundings.

"Come along," said Wiggett, with feigned heartiness, slapping him on the back.

Mr. Miller, looking for a moment as though he would like to return the compliment, came back to everyday life, and bidding the company good-night, stepped to the door, accompanied by his rival. It was immediately shut with some violence.

"They seem in a hurry," said Wiggett. "I don't think I shall go there again."

"I don't think I shall," said Mr. Miller.

After this neither of them was surprised to meet there again the next night, and indeed for several nights. The carpenter and his wife, who did not want the money to go out of the family, and were also afraid of offending Mrs. Pullen, were at their wits' end what to do. Ultimately it was resolved that Tidger, in as delicate a manner as possible, was to hint to her that they were after her money. He was so vague and so delicate that Mrs. Pullen misunderstood him, and fancying that he was trying to borrow half a crown, made him a present of five shillings.

It was evident to the slower-going Mr. Miller that his rival's tongue was giving him an advantage which only the ever-watchful presence of the carpenter and his wife prevented him from pushing to the fullest advantage. In these circumstances he sat for two hours after breakfast one morning in deep cogitation, and after six pipes got up with a twinkle in his slow eyes which his brother dealers had got to regard as a danger signal.

He had only the glimmering of an idea at first, but after a couple of pints at the "Bell" everything took shape, and he cast his eyes about for an assistant. They fell upon a man named Smith, and the dealer, after some thought, took up his glass and went over to him.

"I want you to do something for me," he remarked, in a mysterious voice.

"Ah, I've been wanting to see you," said Smith, who was also a dealer in a small way. "One o' them hins I bought off you last week is dead."

"I'll give you another for it," said Miller.

"And the others are so forgetful," continued Mr. Smith.

"Forgetful?" repeated the other.

"Forget to lay, like," said Mr. Smith, musingly.

"Never mind about them," said Mr. Miller, with some animation. "I want you to do something for me. If it comes off all right, I'll give you a dozen hins and a couple of decentish-sized pigs."

Mr. Smith called a halt. "Decentish-sized" was vague.

"Take your pick," said Mr. Miller. "You know Mrs. Pullen's got two thousand pounds—"

"Wiggett's going to have it," said the other; "he as good as told me so."

"He's after her money," said the other, sadly. "Look 'ere, Smith, I want you to tell him she's lost it all. Say that Tidger told you, but you wasn't to tell anybody else. Wiggett 'll believe you."

Mr. Smith turned upon him a face all wrinkles, lit by one eye. "I want the hins and the pigs first," he said, firmly.

Mr. Miller, shocked at his grasping spirit, stared at him mournfully.

"And twenty pounds the day you marry Mrs. Pullen," continued Mr. Smith.

Mr. Miller, leading him up and down the sawdust floor, besought him to listen to reason, and Mr. Smith allowed the better feelings of our common human nature to prevail to the extent of reducing his demands to half a dozen fowls on account, and all the rest on the day of the marriage. Then, with the delightful feeling that he wouldn't do any work for a week, he went out to drop poison into the ears of Mr. Wiggett.

"Lost all her money!" said the startled Mr. Wiggett. "How?"

"I don't know how," said his friend. "Tidger told me, but made me promise not to tell a soul. But I couldn't help telling you, Wiggett, 'cause I know what you're after."

"Do me a favour," said the little man.

"I will," said the other.

"Keep it from Miller as long as possible. If you hear any one else talking of it, tell 'em to keep it from him. If he marries her I'll give you a couple of pints."

Mr. Smith promised faithfully, and both the Tidgers and Mrs. Pullen were surprised to find that Mr. Miller was the only visitor that evening. He spoke but little, and that little in a slow, ponderous voice intended for Mrs. Pullen's ear alone. He spoke disparagingly of money, and shook his head slowly at the temptations it brought in its train. Give him a crust, he said, and somebody to halve it with —a home-made crust baked by a wife. It was a pretty picture, but somewhat spoiled by Mrs. Tidger suggesting that, though he had spoken of halving the crust, he had said nothing about the beer.

"Half of my beer wouldn't be much," said the dealer, slowly.

"Not the half you would give your wife wouldn't," retorted Mrs. Tidger.

The dealer sighed and looked mournfully at Mrs. Pullen. The lady sighed in return, and finding that her admirer's stock of conversation seemed to be exhausted, coyly suggested a game of draughts. The dealer assented with eagerness, and declining the offer of a glass of beer by explaining that he had had one the day before yesterday, sat down and lost seven games right off. He gave up at the seventh game, and pushing back his chair, said that he thought Mrs. Pullen was the most wonderful draught-player he had ever seen, and took no notice when Mrs. Tidger, in a dry voice charged with subtle meaning, said that she thought he was.

"Draughts come natural to some people," said Mrs. Pullen, modestly. "It's as easy as kissing your fingers."

Mr. Miller looked doubtful; then he put his great fingers to his lips by way of experiment, and let them fall unmistakably in the widow's direction. Mrs. Pullen looked down and nearly blushed. The carpenter and his wife eyed each other in indignant consternation.

"That's easy enough," said the dealer, and repeated the offense.

Mrs. Pullen got up in some confusion, and began to put the draught-board away. One of the pieces fell on the floor, and as they both stooped to recover it their heads bumped. It was nothing to the dealer's, but Mrs. Pullen rubbed hers and sat down with her eyes watering. Mr. Miller took out his handkerchief, and going to the scullery, dipped it into water and held it to her head.

"Is it better?" he inquired.

"A little better," said the victim, with a shiver.

Mr. Miller, in his emotion, was squeezing the handkerchief hard, and a cold stream was running down her neck.

"Thank you.   It's all right now."

The dealer replaced the handkerchief, and sat for some time regarding her earnestly. Then the carpenter and his wife displaying manifest signs of impatience, he took his departure, after first inviting himself for another game of draughts the following night.

He walked home with the air of a conqueror, and thought exultingly that the two thousand pounds were his.   It was a deal after his own heart, and not the least satisfactory part about it was the way he had got the better of Wiggett.

He completed his scheme the following day after a short interview with the useful Smith. By the afternoon Wiggett found that his exclusive information was common property, and all Thatcham was marvelling at the fortitude with which Mrs. Pullen was bearing the loss of her fortune.

With a view of being out of the way when the denial was published, Mr. Miller, after loudly expressing in public his sympathy for Mrs. Pullen and his admiration of her qualities, drove over with some pigs to a neighbouring village, returning to Thatcham in the early evening. Then hurriedly putting his horse up he made his way to the carpenter's.

The Tidgers were at home when he entered, and Mrs. Pullen flushed faintly as he shook hands.

"I was coming in before," he said, impressively, "after what I heard this afternoon, but I had to drive over to Thorpe."

"You 'eard it?" inquired the carpenter, in an incredulous voice.

"Certainly," said the dealer, "and very sorry I was. Sorry for one thing, but glad for another."

The carpenter opened his mouth and seemed about to speak. Then he checked himself suddenly and gazed with interest at the ingenuous dealer.

"I'm glad," said Mr. Miller, slowly, as he nodded at a friend of Mrs. Tidger's who had just come in with a long face, "because now that Mrs. Pullen is poor, I can say to her what I couldn't say while she was rich."

Again the astonished carpenter was about to speak, but the dealer hastily checked him with his hand.

"One at a time," he said. "Mrs. Pullen, I was very sorry to hear this afternoon, for your sake, that you had lost all your money. What I wanted to say to you now, now that you are poor, was to ask you to be Mrs. Miller. What d'ye say?"

Mrs. Pullen, touched at so much goodness, wept softly and said, "Yes." The triumphant Miller took out his handkerchief—the same that he had used the previous night, for he was not an extravagant man—and tenderly wiped her eyes.

"Well, I'm blowed!" said the staring carpenter.

"I've got a nice little 'ouse," continued the wily Mr. Miller. "It's a poor place, but nice, and we'll play draughts every evening. When shall it be?"

"When you like," said Mrs. Pullen, in a faint voice.

"I'll put the banns up to-morrow," said the dealer.

Mrs. Tidger's lady friend giggled at so much haste, but Mrs. Tidger, who felt that she had misjudged him, was touched.

"It does you credit, Mr. Miller," she said, warmly.

"No, no," said the dealer; and then Mr. Tidger got up, and crossing the room, solemnly shook hands with him.

"Money or no money, she'll make a good wife," he said.

"I'm glad you're pleased," said the dealer, wondering at this cordiality.

"I don't deny I thought you was after her money," continued the carpenter, solemnly. "My missus thought so, too."

Mr. Miller shook his head, and said he thought they would have known him better.

"Of course it is a great loss," said the carpenter. "Money is money."

"That's all it is, though," said the slightly mystified Mr. Miller.

"What I can't understand is," continued the carpenter, " 'ow the news got about. Why, the neighbours knew of it a couple of hours before we did."

The dealer hid a grin. Then he looked a bit bewildered again.

"I assure you," said the carpenter, "it was known in the town at least a couple of hours before we got the letter."

Mr. Miller waited a minute to get perfect control over his features. "Letter?" he repeated, faintly.

"The letter from the lawyers," said the carpenter.

Mr. Miller was silent again. His features were getting tiresome. He eyed the door furtively.

"What—was—in—the letter?" he asked.

"Short and sweet," said the carpenter, with bitterness. "Said it was all a mistake, because they'd been and found another will. People shouldn't make such mistakes."

"We're all liable to make mistakes," said Miller, thinking he saw an opening.

"Yes, we made a mistake when we thought you was after Ann's money," assented the carpenter. "I'm sure I thought you'd be the last man in the world to be pleased to hear that she'd lost it. One thing is, you've got enough for both."

"WE'LL LEAVE YOU TWO YOUNG THINGS ALONE."

Mr. Miller made no reply, but in a dazed way strove to realize the full measure of the misfortune which had befallen him. The neighbour, with the anxiety of her sex to be the first with a bit of news, had already taken her departure. He thought of Wiggett walking the earth a free man, and of Smith with a three-months' bill for twenty pounds. His pride as a dealer was shattered beyond repair, and emerging from a species of mist, he became conscious that the carpenter was addressing him.

"We'll leave you two young things alone for a bit," said Mr. Tidger, heartily. "We're going out. When you're tired o' courting you can play draughts, and Ann will show you one or two of 'er moves. So long."

Three at Table

THREE AT TABLE

THE talk in the coffee-room had been of ghosts and apparitions, and nearly everybody present had contributed his mite to the stock of information upon a hazy and somewhat threadbare subject. Opinions ranged from rank incredulity to childlike faith, one believer going so far as to denounce unbelief as impious, with a reference to the Witch of Endor, which was somewhat marred by being complicated in an inexplicable fashion with the story of Jonah.

"Talking of Jonah," he said solemnly, with a happy disregard of the fact that he had declined to answer several eager questions put to him on the subject, "look at the strange tales sailors tell us."

"I wouldn't advise you to believe all those," said a bluff, clean-shaven man, who had been listening without speaking much. "You see when a sailor gets ashore he's expected to have something to tell, and his friends would be rather disappointed if he had not."

"It's a well-known fact," interrupted the first speaker firmly, "that sailors are very prone to see visions."

"They are," said the other dryly, "they generally see them in pairs, and the shock to the nervous system frequently causes headache next morning."

"You never saw anything yourself?" suggested an unbeliever.

"Man and boy," said the other, "I've been at sea thirty years, and the only unpleasant incident of that kind occurred in a quiet English countryside."

"And that?" said another man.

"I was a young man at the time," said the narrator, drawing at his pipe and glancing good-humouredly at the company. "I had just come back from China, and my own people being away I went down into the country to invite myself to stay with an uncle. When I got down to the place I found it closed and the family in the South of France; but as they were due back in a couple of days I decided to put up at the Royal George, a very decent inn, and await their return.

"The first day I passed well enough; but in the evening the dulness of the rambling old place, in which I was the only visitor, began to weigh upon my spirits, and the next morning after a late breakfast I set out with the intention of having a brisk day's walk.

"I started off in excellent spirits, for the day was bright and frosty, with a powdering of snow on the iron-bound roads and nipped hedges, and the country had to me all the charm of novelty. It was certainly flat, but there was plenty of timber, and the villages through which I passed were old and picturesque.

"I lunched luxuriously on bread and cheese and beer in the bar of a small inn, and resolved to go a little further before turning back. When at length I found I had gone far enough, I turned up a lane at right angles to the road I was passing, and resolved to find my way back by another route. It is a long lane that has no turning, but this had several, each of which had turnings of its own, which generally led, as I found by trying two or three of them, into the open marshes. Then, tired of lanes, I resolved to rely upon the small compass which hung from my watch chain and go across country home.

"I had got well into the marshes when a white fog, which had been for some time hovering round the edge of the ditches, began gradually to spread. There was no escaping it, but by aid of my compass I was saved from making a circular tour and fell instead into frozen ditches or stumbled over roots in the grass. I kept my course, however, until at four o'clock, when night was coming rapidly up to lend a hand to the fog, I was fain to confess myself lost.

"The compass was now no good to me, and I wandered about miserably, occasionally giving a shout on the chance of being heard by some passing shepherd or farmhand. At length by great good luck I found my feet on a rough road driven through the marshes, and by walking slowly and tapping with my stick managed to keep to it. I had followed it for some distance when I heard footsteps approaching me.

"We stopped as we met, and the new arrival, a sturdy-looking countryman, hearing of my plight, walked back with me for nearly a mile, and putting me on to a road gave me minute instructions how to reach a village some three miles distant.

"I was so tired that three miles sounded like ten, and besides that, a little way off from the road I saw dimly a lighted window.   I pointed it out, but my companion shuddered and looked round him uneasily.

" 'You won't get no good there,' he said, hastily.

" 'Why not?' I asked.

" 'There's a something there, sir,' he replied, 'what 'tis I dunno, but the little 'un belonging to a gamekeeper as used to live in these parts see it, and it was never much good afterward. Some say as it's a poor mad thing, others says as it's a kind of animal; but whatever it is, it ain't good to see.'

" 'Well, I'll keep on, then,' I said.   'Good-night.'

"He went back whistling cheerily until his footsteps died away in the distance, and I followed the road he had indicated until it divided into three, any one of which to a stranger might be said to lead straight on. I was now cold and tired, and having half made up my mind walked slowly back toward the house.

"At first all I could see of it was the little patch of light at the window. I made for that until it disappeared suddenly, and I found myself walking into a tall hedge. I felt my way round this until I came to a small gate, and opening it cautiously, walked, not without some little nervousness, up a long path which led to the door. There was no light and no sound from within. Half repenting of my temerity I shortened my stick and knocked lightly upon the door.

"I waited a couple of minutes and then knocked again, and my stick was still beating the door when it opened suddenly and a tall bony old woman, holding a candle, confronted me.

"'What do you want?' she demanded gruffly.

"'I've lost my way,' I said, civilly; 'I want to get to Ashville.'

" 'Don't know it,' said the old woman.

"She was about to close the door when a man emerged from a room at the side of the hall and came toward us. An old man of great height and breadth of shoulder.

" 'Ashville is fifteen miles distant,' he said slowly.

" 'If you will direct me to the nearest village, I shall be grateful,' I remarked.

"He made no reply, but exchanged a quick, furtive glance with the woman. She made a gesture of dissent.

" 'The nearest place is three miles off,' he said, turning to me and apparently trying to soften a naturally harsh voice; 'if you will give me the pleasure of your company, I will make you as comfortable as I can.'

"I hesitated. They were certainly a queer-looking couple, and the gloomy hall with the shadows thrown by the candle looked hardly more inviting than the darkness outside.

" 'You are very kind,' I murmured, irresolutely, 'but——'

" 'Come in,' he said quickly; 'shut the door, Anne.'

"Almost before I knew it I was standing inside and the old woman, muttering to herself, had closed the door behind me. With a queer sensation of being trapped I followed my host into the room, and taking the proffered chair warmed my frozen fingers at the fire. ·

" 'Dinner will soon be ready,' said the old man, regarding me closely. 'If you will excuse me——'

"I bowed and he left the room. A minute afterward I heard voices; his and the old woman's, and, I fancied, a third. Before I had finished my inspection of the room he returned, and regarded me with the same strange look I had noticed before.

" 'There will be three of us at dinner,' he said, at length. 'We two and my son.'

"I bowed again, and secretly hoped that that look didn't run in the family.

" 'I suppose you don't mind dining in the dark,' he said, abruptly.

" 'Not at all,' I replied, hiding my surprise as well as I could, 'but really I'm afraid I'm intruding. If you'll allow me——'

"He waved his huge gaunt hands. 'We're

not going to lose you now we've got you,' he said, with a dry laugh. 'It's seldom we have company, and now we've got you we'll keep you. My son's eyes are bad, and he can't stand the light. Ah, here is Anne.'

"As he spoke the old woman entered, and, eyeing me stealthily, began to lay the cloth, while my host, taking a chair the other side of the hearth, sat looking silently into the fire. The table set, the old woman brought in a pair of fowls ready carved in a dish, and placing three chairs, left the room. The old man hesitated a moment, and then, rising from his chair, placed a large screen in front of the fire and slowly extinguished the candles.

" 'Blind man's holiday,' he said, with clumsy jocosity, and groping his way to the door opened it. Somebody came back into the room with him, and in a slow, uncertain fashion took a seat at the table, and the strangest voice I have ever heard broke a silence which was fast becoming oppressive.

" 'A cold night,' it said slowly.

"I replied in the affirmative, and light or no light, fell to with an appetite which had only been sharpened by the snack in the middle of the day. It was somewhat difficult eating in the dark, and it was evident from the behaviour of my invisible companions that they were as unused to dining under such circumstances as I was. We ate in silence until the old woman blundered into the room with some sweets and put them with a crash upon the table.

" 'Are you a stranger about here?' inquired the curious voice again.

"I replied in the affirmative, and murmured something about my luck in stumbling upon such a good dinner.

" 'Stumbling is a very good word for it,' said the voice grimly. 'You have forgotten the port, father.'

" 'So I have,' said the old man, rising. 'It's a bottle of the "Celebrated" to-day; I will get it myself.'

"He felt his way to the door, and closing it behind him, left me alone with my unseen neighbour. There was something so strange about the whole business that I must confess to more than a slight feeling of uneasiness.

"My host seemed to be absent a long time. I heard the man opposite lay down his fork and spoon, and half fancied I could see a pair of wild eyes shining through the gloom like a cat's.

"With a growing sense of uneasiness I pushed my chair back. It caught the hearth-rug, and in my efforts to disentangle it the screen fell over with a crash and in the flickering light of the fire I saw the face of the creature opposite. With a sharp catch of my breath I left my chair and stood with clenched fists beside it. Man or beast, which was it? The flame leaped up and then went out, and in the mere red glow of the fire it looked more devilish than before.

"For a few moments we regarded each other in silence; then the door opened and the old man returned. He stood aghast as he saw the warm firelight, and then approaching the table mechanically put down a couple of bottles.

" 'I beg your pardon,' said I, reassured by his presence, 'but I have accidentally overturned the screen. Allow me to replace it.'

" 'No,' said the old man, gently, 'let it be.

We have had enough of the dark. I'll give you a light.'

"He struck a match and slowly lit the candles. Then I saw that the man opposite had but the remnant of a face, a gaunt wolfish face in which one unquenched eye, the sole remaining feature, still glittered. I was greatly moved, some suspicion of the truth occurring to me.

" 'My son was injured some years ago in a burning house,' said the old man. 'Since then we have lived a very retired life. When you came to the door we——' his voice trembled, 'that is—my son——'

" 'I thought,' said the son simply, 'that it would be better for me not to come to the dinner-table. But it happens to be my birthday, and my father would not hear of my dining alone, so we hit upon this foolish plan of dining in the dark. I'm sorry I startled you.'

" 'I am sorry,' said I, as I reached across the table and gripped his hand, 'that I am such a fool; but it was only in the dark that you startled me.'

"From a faint tinge in the old man's cheek

and a certain pleasant softening of the poor solitary eye in front of me I secretly congratulated myself upon this last remark.

" 'We never see a friend,' said the old man, apologetically, 'and the temptation to have company was too much for us. Besides, I don't know what else you could have done.'

" 'Nothing else half so good, I'm sure,' said I.

" 'Come,' said my host, with almost a sprightly air. 'Now we know each other, draw your chairs to the fire and let's keep this birthday in a proper fashion.'

"He drew a small table to the fire for the glasses and produced a box of cigars, and placing a chair for the old servant, sternly bade her to sit down and drink. If the talk was not sparkling, it did not lack for vivacity, and we were soon as merry a party as I have ever seen. The night wore on so rapidly that we could hardly believe our ears when in a lull in the conversation a clock in the hall struck twelve.

" 'A last toast before we retire,' said my host, pitching the end of his cigar into the fire and turning to the small table.

"We had drunk several before this, but there was something impressive in the old man's manner as he rose and took up his glass.   His tall figure seemed to get taller, and his voice rang as he gazed proudly at his disfigured son.

" 'The health of the children my boy saved!' he said, and drained his glass at a draught."

THE END.

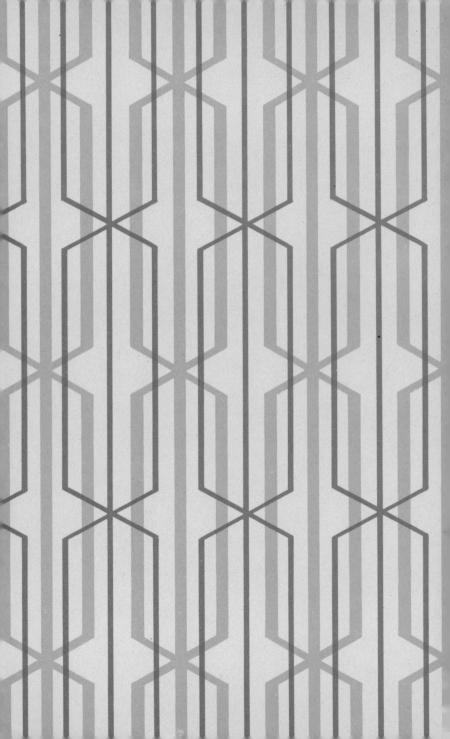